OF STARDUST
LORE RESHAPED
AVRAH C. BAREN

CHAOS MONSTER PUBLISHING

Cover design © Fantastical Ink

Edited by Lillian Barry

Published by Chaos Monster Publishing LLC

ISBN 9798990054653 (paperback)

ISBN 9798990054646 (ebook)

CONTENTS

For those of us fighting to make room for ourselves in worlds
both real and fictional.
Keep fighting.
We will too.

To everyone who backed our anthology on Kickstarter, thank
you for helping us put more queer magic out in the world.

PREFACE

Walking around Washington DC in the late spring of 2025 has felt like waiting for the next gut punch to hit day after day. So when a friend invited a few of us to their house for a potluck "just because", none of us were in a particularly joyful mood. We were grateful to gather and nurse our wounds among friends, to make soup and cornbread and feast on community and togetherness. And then, our host asked us to share something we were excited about.

A resounding silence.

I won't project onto others, but I know I was thinking about the friends who had been fired from government jobs. About how my once stable career felt like it was now teetering on the edge of collapse. About the anti-trans legislation rolling out in waves across the US, denying basic human rights to a marginalized community that has only ever asked for the right to exist without fear. About ICE raids tearing people from their homes without empathy or any sense of morality. About the wrongful deportation of university students and the disingenuous claims of Antisemitism—a real and active threat—to justify those deportations, push a xenophobic agenda, and all the while add fuel to *actual* Antisemitism. All I could see for those few moments of silence were all the things rich men in power had done to inflict violence upon real people they were treating like numbers to be managed.

And then someone shared that they'd seen the sun shine that day and how they were excited winter was nearly over. Someone spoke about taking a really great nap when they needed it. Another person had been able to enjoy Iftar with a friend. I remembered that I was getting ready to see writing friends and breathe fresh mountain air. We remembered we were taking trips to visit people we loved. That all of us still had something, even a glimmer of hope, to celebrate. To fight for.

The concept that joy is an act of resistance has long been cherished in activist spaces. Joy feels elusive when basic human rights are being attacked. But joy is what gives us something to get out of bed for, to rally around. A positive motion of fighting *for* something, not just the difficulty of fighting *against* something. Joy gives us the strength to fight for the idea that things can and should be better. That we can shape the world into a safer place.

Of the stories you will find in this collection, many are contemplative, the joy in them hiding below the surface. But to me, there is a joy that comes from knowing that each story features a world where queer people in all their myriad forms have a home. Every word within these pages will hold open the door to a world we want to see. These stories take tales that have for too long painted a very specific view of reality and shines new light on them. They imagine our past, present, and future the way it has, is, and will always be: queer.

Joy, especially queer joy, may feel unfathomable right now. But I promise you it's there. If I have learned nothing else since January 2025, it's that queer people have always been adept at forming community. We've had to be. And those communities are vital at this moment. Friends, loved ones, people who hold us up remind us that we have things to be excited about, that we have something to work towards: a world where each and every one of us can live safe, fulfilling, and joyful lives.

I refuse to stop imagining that world. So in those moments when I'm sitting around a table of friends, struggling to think of anything to be excited about, I will make myself remember what I love about life, and what I love about my queerness. I'll remember that I saw a blue jay land on my windowsill today. That despite how skittish she is, my cat will let me shove my face in her belly about twice a day. That I have friends who send me flowers and feed me when I'm grieving. I will hold onto all of these things. I will get out bed every day. And I will keep fighting.

To exist as a queer person is fight enough. Maybe your fight looks like attending protests. Maybe it's just making sure you've had enough water today. And maybe it's reading this book to fill your well with stories of star-crossed lovers and hungry balete trees, of rusalkas and androids and so much more.

No matter what your fight looks like, I wish you the joy we all deserve.

She Never Turned

Avrah C. Baren

When Orpheus's foot paused at the foot of that last step, when he made that slow turn over his shoulder, when his eyes caught on those of his lover's, who'd followed him out of death, who'd trusted him all that long, dark walk, a thousand poets lifted their pens and put ink to paper. One small glance, a mistake perhaps, and his story became legend for the world to salivate over for millennia to come. For future artists to revel in the tragedy of it. A happy reunion had been his for the taking, yet doubt had consumed him. Had tilted his head until he could not help but look back and doom his beloved Eurydice to her final death.

And what of the lover doomed to her fate in Hades?

What about me?

More than the look of terror on Orpheus's face, more than the last glimpse of the ethereal face of the muse's son, I remember the sun. Warm and golden on my skin. The breath of Life hot on my face. Torn away as his eyes met mine and the doorway closed and I was flung down, down, down into Hades.

Swept along with the tide of the Styx and regurgitated onto the obsidian of the throne room. No gentle ushering of Charon and his skiff made of waterworn bone. A rush of water, the cold of death, and then I lay in a heap before the thrones of King Aidoneus and Persephone, his queen of death and rebirth.

I shivered and did not move, black water dripping from my dress onto blacker stones. In death the cold could not reach me. And yet the sun. The sun.

Time moves strangely in the underworld. I might have lain there mere moments or years, so long as to become one of the statues of heroes arrayed about the reception hall. Long enough that my skin, which had turned a healthy olive as I neared the surface, now returned to the gray of death.

After a time, Queen Persephone took pity on me. Noble shoulders thrown back, spring-green eyes merciful, she rose from her throne and came to my side.

"He failed you, then," she said.

I made no response. The sun was still on my skin. I could feel it, taste it. How I ached for its golden glow.

The queen held out her hand, smooth as marble, brown as the fertile earth she walks each spring. And I took it, too numb to wonder over a queen, a goddess, bending down to help a wretched heap of a human, a dead one at that, off the ground.

She squeezed my shoulder, the whisper of Life echoing her touch, and I leaned into it.

"It's alright, child," she murmured for my ears alone. "Men so often do."

I remembered the ballads of her abduction. How her father had conspired with his brother to secure her marriage and confinement. Half of her eternal life to be spent underground, starved of warmth and light.

At least she *may breathe freely each spring.* An ungrateful thought I kept to myself.

"Go now," she told me. "Find your peace amidst the fields of Asphodel."

Peace. I could have laughed. Or wailed. How was I to find peace when my second chance at life had been torn away by one man's wavering?

Still, I bowed and made to leave the throne room, which echoed of coins placed upon eyelids.

As I passed between obsidian columns, a figure approached. She hauled a mortal, bound in chains, towards the audience of the underworld's monarchs. Tall as any man, she boasted muscles to rival even the great Heracles. Golden skin and hair the white of Charon's boat. Upon her brow rested a diadem wrought in the shape of two snakes twisting around each other. She spared me a glance with those cruel, silver eyes before tugging hard on the chain.

The man struggled against his confines. Babbled nonsense about his innocence. But if the Erinys Megaera comes for your life, there is no escape. The embodiment of the blade that follows a broken oath. No sweet fields of grain would await this man.

When she passed, heat from her journey aboveground made me shudder, as if a star grazed my skin.

Though she paid me no mind, I followed her with my eyes, watched with grim relish as she threw the man to the ground at King Aidoneus's feet.

As his sentence was proclaimed, warm satisfaction lit me from the inside out.

————◈————

I found her cleaning her sword by the waters of her father, the Acheron. The muscles of her arms moved like rocks beneath the river as she worked. She'd discarded her leather breastplate and gauntlets, but her every movement cut like the blade in her hands, no less dangerous for her lack of adornments.

She did not look up from her work as I stood before her, clasping and unclasping my hands. But with the voice of a river's daughter, she spoke.

"You ask me to seek your vengeance."

I swallowed. Forced myself to clench my hands into stillness by my sides. "Yes."

"Against your muse's son."

I fumbled with the words to tell her that he wasn't mine, not anymore. But in the end it mattered not.

"Yes."

She sighed and finally met my gaze. "I do not take my work lightly, mortal. Your poet made a bargain for your life. The bargain is complete. He returned to the surface; you returned to death. I cannot take his life when there are so many others more deserving of the blade."

And yet I could not forget the heat of the sun. How I would only ever be remembered as a wife who lived an obscure life and died a tragic death. Songs dedicated to me, but only as an object defined by the life of a man.

"My chance was taken from me," I told her, trying to disguise my trembling. "It was held in his hands. I had no control of my life, not even when given another chance at it. Please. Allow me some control in my death."

She eyed me, those silver eyes piercing to the quick, sharp as the fangs of a viper. "Hmm."

I tried to be patient, but when she held her silence, I broke. "Please, Megaera. Hades's Fury. Give me this."

"And what will you give me in return?" she asked, sheathing her blade.

"I-I—" My mind stuttered to a halt. I was dead. I had nothing but the clothes on my back. The tendrils of black hair on my head. The two gold coins gifted upon my death already spent to secure Charon's skiff.

"How about we make a bargain of our own?" she said, something like mischief lighting her cold eyes.

"What sort of bargain?"

I'd had enough bargains to last an eternity of wandering Asphodel. But I remembered the man's blubbering at the feet of a king. How the suffering he'd caused another had been mirrored back onto him. And it felt like a sunbeam straight through my heart.

"I will teach you how to hold a sword. How to brandish it without bringing shame to the blade. Even lend you the token you will need to return to the earth to take vengeance yourself."

I had spun enough myths into song in my short lifetime to know when the second edge of her beautiful sword would be revealed. She sharpened it so kindly. With a smile.

"And in exchange," she said, merciful enough to make the blow swift for all her ferocity, "you will write me a song."

I could not help but gawk. "A song?"

Her nod was all seriousness. Still I wondered if I mistook the sparkle in her eye. "A song."

The laugh that emerged was not a kind one. "You need not stuff my wounds with salt. The poet has returned to the surface."

She raised a brow.

A song. A trifle to her eyes. And yet...

"Why?" I asked, suspicious.

She shrugged. "I've never had a song written for me. Just me. Not one of a trio of Erinys. I should like it, I think."

My chest no longer held a beating heart. Still, it managed to twist and writhe between my bones. The memory of fingers on the strings of a lyre. My head leaned back against Orpheus's thigh as he plucked one string and then another. The frustrated mutterings when it was not to his liking.

She could not know how deeply her request cut. More than a fair bargain in her eyes.

And so, when she held out her hand, I shook it. "Alright. Then a song you shall have."

If I could write one.

—◈—

The first I ever laid eyes on Orpheus, it was not his looks, spindly and gossamer as they were, that drew me to him, but his voice. Those long fingers plucking the lyre.

How we would sing together, him ever the patient teacher as I tried to demonstrate my own skill with the lyre, my own voice. Until I grew weary of his corrections. Until I accepted that it was he who was the talent, and I the muse, a fate as inevitable as the turning of his head when he doubted me that final time.

Still, a song required a tune, and I was not so unpracticed even now. I crept through the audience chamber to make my request after all other petitioners had fled and Aidoneus's towering throne sat empty. Only Queen Persephone remained, chin nestled on her hand, warm eyes glimmering as I made my hesitant approach and bowed before her.

When I begged a lyre of the queen of the underworld, she gave me a sad smile and led me to a room of glorious instruments, those left by the great poets who had passed before Aidoneus's judgment. As she placed her hand on the instrument in question, I nearly swallowed my tongue.

It was a divine thing, carved with the scenes of gods in their might, corded with rivers of gold.

When I tried to refuse the piece, Persephone would hear none of it.

"What use is such a treasure if it gathers dust? Take it. There is little music of late in my husband's realm. I would welcome your using it."

With trembling hands, I took the instrument to the riverside, and for the first time in years, ran my fingers along the strings of a lyre.

I meant to begin the work immediately, to spin up words that would secure my end of Megaera's bargain before I could regret our deal.

Instead, I played until my fingers bled and tears had soaked my chiton through.

———◆———

Calluses brought along by playing the lyre were nothing compared to those needed to wield a sword, even a practice one.

And Megaera was no gentle teacher.

"Again," she said, urging me to hold the wooden sword aloft, no matter my aching arms. It seemed even in death, my body had its limits.

I gripped the hilt, ignoring the scream of my muscles. Lifted the sword. And followed Megaera's lead through the motions of strikes and blocks. My body urged me to protest that she was pushing me too hard, that I had been raised for tasks befitting a maiden and then a wife, not swordplay.

But there was a look in her eye that kept such words firmly trapped in my throat. Resolution. Belief. That if I would pick up the sword, she could teach me to wield it. And if she could teach me to wield it, I would be fit to bear it with pride.

I swung the sword in a now familiar arc. Met by the less familiar jolt as her wooden sword struck out and knocked mine from my hands.

"You understand the forms. Now, you must learn to read an opponent. To improvise. You must become crafty as well as strong."

I stumbled over to retrieve my sword on shaky legs. "Orpheus is no more a warrior than myself. Surely the forms will be enough."

"And will you be satisfied when you cut down your poet who knows nothing of war?"

I grimaced. "It will be only as he deserves for stealing my chance at life."

"Is that all he stole?" Megaera asked, silver eyes glinting.

The question caught me off guard, made my chest go tight. "What do you mean?"

She shrugged. "Now, tell me, how goes my song?"

I shouldered the wooden sword, savoring what respite I could gain from the conversation. "It goes..." I'd meant to lie and found I could not. I sighed. "I'm finding it difficult."

Megaera mirrored my position. "How so? I hear you strumming your borrowed lyre. You have no lack of skill."

"It is not my skill, it is...it's you," I admitted.

Silver eyes glittered, light eyebrows rising up in surprise. "Me?"

"I know so very little about you."

A scoff. "Has the mortal world forgotten me and my sisters so easily?"

"No, no, you are beings of legend," I insisted. "I know all the tales. Of Sisyphus and Orestes. How you and your sisters exact the punishment of the gods. But you. You I hardly know. How do I write a song about someone I barely know?"

"Your poet managed just fine."

The barb stung, wedged itself under my skin and tore. "I know. But I always found such songs..."

"What?" she encouraged.

"Lacking."

"I see."

For a moment, we stood in silence. I wondered if I'd said too much, overstepped in my judgment of what and what was not a song worth writing.

Eventually she nodded. "Then we will continue to train. And I will tell you more of myself if you wish it."

And I did. More than I had ever wished to know another living soul.

"Now," she said, leveling her sword at me, "I shall show you how to block a real strike, little Fury."

———◈———

When Megaera was summoned to retrieve some vicious soul or another, I was left to my own devices in Asphodel. Amid the endless sea of wheat, I lost myself in the strumming of the lyre. Of finding a voice all my own. No husband to call it wrong or demonstrate how his songs would always be superior.

Once, settled in a quiet corner, struggling to bead words together into a song worthy of the great Megaera, another wandering soul came, called by my music. A woman whose face was worn by time so that her features were nearly washed clean. I wondered if all the dead of Asphodel looked like that after a time. When my own face would lose all features. If Megaera would remember it when all living souls had forgotten it.

The woman knelt before me, listening to my playing in silence for a while, until I turned my fingers to a song of old. And when she spoke, the words stirred embers in my belly.

"That song. I know it. The great poet Orpheus played it when I was living," she said with a voice that sounded like rain washing down a rock face.

I stopped my playing, gripping the lyre so hard I thought I might break it. For a moment I considered smashing the beautiful thing to ruins.

"No," I gritted out. "This song is mine."

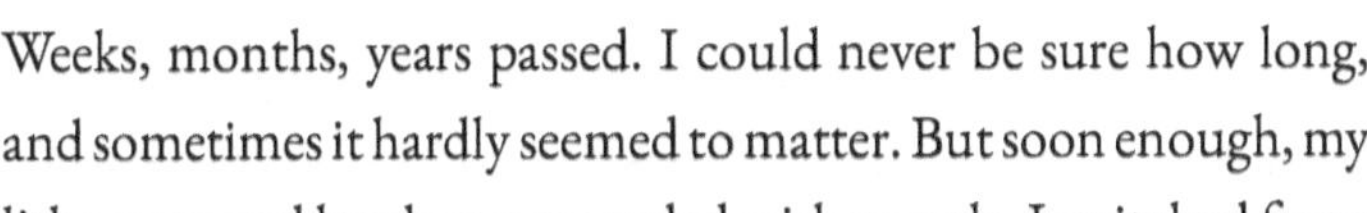

Weeks, months, years passed. I could never be sure how long, and sometimes it hardly seemed to matter. But soon enough, my lithe arms and legs became corded with muscle. I switched from the wooden practice sword to a blunt xiphos of heavy iron.

Megaera and I began to spar. I never bested her. I never expected to. But little by little I began to unravel her like a tapestry I could piece together again when the time was right.

She spoke of her love for her mother, the night. The way she had always craved the feeling of an iron blade in her hand. The satisfaction she felt each time she balanced the scale and exacted vengeance upon the adulterers and oath breakers of the mortal world. How despite an immortal life of violence she had always felt drawn to music. The disappointment of how wrong an instrument felt in her hands paired with the delight of a ballad in her ears.

In return, I recounted the stories my mother had told me of my own origins. My own skepticism as a child when she refused to explain just how the god Apollo could have fathered me. The terrible understanding as I grew older. How I had always loved singing to greet Persephone's spring, convinced that my voice would aid her in encouraging buds to bloom. How for years it was only myself and my mother and my voice. My confusion as to why I had ever stopped singing.

I grew stronger, faster. Not quite a warrior, nor one of the Erinys, but something my own. My voice returned.

As we worked, our togetherness began spilling into all corners of my death. The exchanging of blows followed by strolls along the Acheron, Megaera's silver gaze a constant heat on my skin. By the sharing of tales old and new as the golden fields of Asphodel swayed to the silent breeze. Her fingers were no longer confined to touching only when my form with the sword required correction, and now found more excuses to thread through mine, even when they were empty.

Meg stopped asking about Orpheus.

But I never forgot.

⸻ ❖ ⸻

"Your song is ready," I told her one day.

"Oh?" I was surprised by the disappointment in her eyes. And my own hurt in response.

I took the blade from her hand and set it aside, holding both her hands in mine, turning them over to observe each and every callus. She shivered as I ran a thumb over her knuckles. I worried it was the cold of my skin and made to let go, but she stopped me.

Her grip reassured me as I voiced my confusion. "I thought you wished me to write a song just for you."

Those silver eyes piercing into mine. "What if perhaps I only wished to hear you sing?"

I chuckled. "My voice has gone to cobwebs, much like my tomb above."

"I doubt that," she murmured, leaning so close I could feel the heat of her skin, still warm from her last trip above.

"First you wanted a song, and now you want my voice?" I meant to tease her, but bitterness turned the words sour. "I told you before, Orpheus is the poet. I'm just—"

"His muse?"

I froze, tearing my gaze away. Until her fingers gently turned my chin to face her. "Eurydice, whose songs did your Orpheus sing?"

Years stretching on and on. A lyre pulled from my hands and replaced with needle and thread. Orpheus's promise that though our world had no room for a female poet, I would be forever remembered when he sang.

Mine, I ached to cry. *Those songs were mine.*

My words. My tunes. His voice. His name.

And I'd promised not to tell a soul for fear that knowing a woman could write such music would cause each song to be struck from history.

"How did you know?" I whispered.

"Even oaths not spoken aloud can be broken," she murmured sadly. "Stealing another's music is still a betrayal, even if not a fatal one. And so I have always known, little songbird who would be a Fury."

It struck me like fangs the way she saw me. Through me. All this time.

"I told myself it was enough," I murmured. "That if the songs were sung, if they were released into the world by someone people would acknowledge as a genius, it was enough."

"And was it?"

I shook my head, blinking back tears. Of course it hadn't been enough. Not when Orpheus had convinced me of my own mediocrity, had turned from the doting husband to the jealous songwriter when my songs received higher praise and louder applause, even though they came from his mouth.

"No," I whispered.

He had stolen not only my chance at life, but also my belief in my own talent. My music. Everything.

This is the way of the world, the way of men, I thought, as if it might bring a shred of comfort.

It was the truth.

And it was wrong.

"If you know all this, why do you hesitate to release me of my bargain?" I asked at last. "Why not hear my song?"

She sighed, a pitying sound. "Because vengeance is sweet for a Fury. And so very bitter for a poet."

I pulled away from her grip, wrapping my arms around myself. "My life is a bitter, wasted thing. What more would the blood on my hands hurt?"

The Fury had no answer. And so I turned my back on her.

I never looked back.

This time when I came to beg audience with Persephone, I came eager, my head held high. The queen had been kind to me, in a sad sort of way. Perhaps she would intercede on my behalf. I knew it was too much to beg for my life again, but for this piece of solace perhaps...

I stepped between obsidian columns. A hand came to my wrist. Gentle but resolute.

Turning in Meg's arms, I allowed myself at last to feel the hope I had pretended away. That she would change her mind. That it would be she who would release me from my pain. When she tugged me away from the edge of the throne room, I followed.

In a darkened alcove, she reached into the pocket of her belt and produced a sprig of heliotrope. Even cut, the white flowers seemed drawn upwards, towards the sun, just as their namesake had wasted away for want of Helios's love. With care far exceeding what I would have expected from such hardened hands, she tucked it behind my ear.

"This will see you safe to the surface."

And now, she handed me a xiphos, displaying its sharpened edge before sheathing it and belting it to my waist.

"And this will see you to your vengeance."

My throat went dry. "But what of your song?"

She smiled. An expression so sad it would have broken my heart had I still possessed one.

"This token will not bring you back to life. You will only have until it begins to wilt. And so I will see you far sooner than perhaps you would like. Will you sing it to me then?"

I took her hands in mine. Pressed my lips to the knuckles at the back of each strong hand.

"I promise."

"Good. Now go. But Eurydice, I will ask you one more question."

"And what's that?" I whispered, chest tight.

"Orpheus and his stolen music. Is he worth all this torment? Is he worth another moment of your death?"

I closed my eyes and swallowed my pain. "No, Meg. But I will be vindicated all the same."

⸻◈⸻

Across the Styx. Through the gate and past Cerberus's ever watchful gaze with no more than a curious sniff in my direction.

Then finally the long, long climb up the stairs.

There was no Orpheus to guide me. No terror dogging my steps that at any moment he would turn around and I would be doomed to death. No disappointment and despair when he did just that. I made my own way out of Hades. And the heat of Life, of the sun, was all the sweeter for it.

I longed to lie down in the grassy field and soak in the warmth. But the flowers were already dying against the thin shell of my ear.

I moved on.

Orpheus was never without an audience, so when I found him, he was seated upon a rock in a grassy glen, folk arrayed in a circle around him, everyone vying for a closer look at the famous poet. The muse's son who needed a muse of his own to write anything worth listening to.

The melody he played now was a sad, slow thing. I recognized it. Because of course, I had written it.

I moved through the seated crowd, and everywhere I walked, people shied away from the cold of Hades on my skin. Little gasps followed my footfall. Until even Orpheus, rapturous and lost in his song, broke off to look at me.

Horror in those blue eyes. They welled with tears, which spilled down his face beautifully. Truth. Or poetry.

"Eurydice," he whispered. "I'm dreaming."

I unsheathed my blade, gripped the xiphos just as Meg had shown me. And when I touched the point of the blade to Orpheus's vulnerable throat, he shivered. I drew the tiniest bead of blood and he flinched. Behind me his audience began tripping over themselves to flee from the violence in the air.

"No. Not a dream, husband of mine. A vengeful ghost."

His lip trembled and he clasped his hands in supplication. "I thought it one of Hades's tricks. That he would make me leave you behind and I would not know until it was too late. I had to know! My love—"

"The song you were playing just now. How did you come by such a sweet melody?"

His brows knit in confusion. "I-I cannot say. The muses spoke in my ear. I have been blessed with their love."

"And what of me?"

"Well, of course all my work is inspired by you. How could it not be? The muses have always smiled upon me, but you have been the most glorious muse of them all! Eurydice how my heart aches to see you here and yet know you are dead!"

"That. Song. Is. Mine," I bit out, pressing the blade harder. Perhaps he had convinced himself that my songwriting was his inspiration. That he was within his rights to take what I had created as my husband and my keeper. That I was owed no credit.

But his music, the music lauded across Gaia's green surface, was mine. Just mine.

"I am so much more than your muse," I hissed.

His throat bobbed against the blade. "Eurydice, please."

I stepped in to deal the final blow. So easy to slice through such soft flesh. To rip stolen music from his throat.

Tittering voices emerged from the clearing, so incongruous to the vengeance at my hands.

I turned, finding the grassy glade empty of Orpheus's adoring fans. Instead, a group of Maenads had emerged, each carrying a jar of wine. Dionysus's worshipers coming in search of revelry.

The women approached, cheeks red and eyes glazed. The fabric of their peploses swayed with each step, already eager for the dance they sought.

One woman, an older Maenad with long black hair, streaked with silver and wild as a storm cloud, giggled into her hand. "How lucky are we to have found the famous Orpheus at his lyre! Come, dear poet, will you not strike up a glad tune so we may dance?"

Orpheus stared at her, then flicked his eyes back to the sword at his neck. "Perhaps now is not the time."

I considered the woman. Her indifference to the mortal danger her desired poet was in. Given the stories I had heard of Maenads and their frenzied violence, it did little to surprise me.

"I could give you a quick death," I told Orpheus. "Or you too could suffer a while."

When I sheathed my sword, Orpheus sputtered, startled.

"Come now, great poet," I said with an exaggerated bow. "Play something fit for a dance."

He swallowed loudly, eyes darting between myself and the Maenad. "I only know songs of sorrow, I'm afraid. Songs I sing to honor the loss of my wife," he added, with a pointed look in my direction.

The Maenad drank from her jar, wine dribbling down her chin until she'd emptied the contents and threw the jar aside.

"That won't do," she said. "Come, sisters, perhaps we can encourage him to change his tune."

"No—I—Eurydice—"

Orpheus had never written a song befitting the sort of dance a Maenad sought. And without my help, he never would.

I took a step backwards, allowing the Maenads to pass. To kneel at Orpheus's side and flirt with him. Then cajole. Then threaten.

Another step. The flower by my ear was wilting. Hades was calling me home. Silver eyes and golden skin awaited me, warmer than even the sun.

"Eurydice!" Orpheus cried as a Maenad grabbed his arm and gnashed her teeth at him.

I turned away from the glade, from my husband and his stolen music.

When he began to scream, I looked over my shoulder and watched the Maenads tear him apart.

She was waiting for me at the entrance to Hades. This time it was not an unwilling soul she would bring below, but someone ready to take her hand and hold tight.

Those silver eyes roved my face, my hands. Checking for hurts, or perhaps the stain of blood.

"Tell me, did you accomplish the vengeance you sought?"

I unstrapped the sword from my belt and placed it into her hands. "You will not need to clean it."

She raised a brow. "And yet his soul descends even now."

I shrugged. "Not by my hand. Perhaps if he had written his own music and gained valor without stealing mine, it would have ended differently. But the Maenads were not pleased with him. I simply...stayed out of their way."

Meg snorted and belted the sword. "You are vicious, for a poet."

"And yet I have heard that words cut sharper than knives," I replied with a grin.

This time she laughed, head thrown back with an ease that made my cheeks warm.

The laughter still tinted her voice when she asked, "So have you chosen to find your joy in your music or the blade?"

I took her hand in mine. "I think I find great joy in both."

Her grin widened. "That is good then, for you have a great talent with either. Come. Shall we go home?"

We walked the whole way hand in hand. And when we sat beside the Acheron, I opened my mouth.

And I sang.

FULL OF GRACE
ROSE REGEANT

Carter really fucked up this time.

She's been hunting fallen angels long enough to know that every hunter meets their end like this—staring up into the rabid red eyes of the fallen angel. Still, she doesn't feel ready. She's got so much more to do. So much more to atone for.

Thunder cracks as claws close around her neck. Lightning strobes through the filthy hotel room, lighting up the decaying visage of the creature that will surely end her life. She stretches out her arm, a desperate reach for the dagger she dropped when the thing ambushed her. Her fingers brush the crucifix-shaped hilt. It's just out of her grasp.

She only has another minute or so before she blacks out from lack of oxygen. She needs a new plan.

Instead of going for the weapon again, Carter grips the angel's bony wrists and tries to crush them in her hands, but they don't shatter. Don't budge from her throat. Otherworldly creatures can easily overpower humans, no matter how delicate they look.

Carter kicks at the floor, bucks her hips, trying to dislodge the vile thing that has her pinned to the stained hotel carpet, but she knows this is a losing game. She shouldn't have gotten so cocky.

The angel hisses as Carter struggles for breath, but not even a modicum of air makes it through her blocked windpipe. The crooked fingers around her neck burn with hellfire. Her vision fogs like the rain-streaked windows. Blood beats in her ears. Her heels slip on the floor. She's going to die.

She's going to die before she makes up for—

Something wet and warm splatters her face just as another whip of lightning thrashes over the scene. The creature screeches, but thunder smothers the sound. Its hands slacken and Carter rakes in a grateful breath at the same moment blood pours from the angel's mouth, and all Carter can think is *I just had this shirt dry cleaned.*

The angel rears back, red spraying across the dingy hotel room walls and a blade of pure light—a blade Carter isn't holding—withdraws from its chest. Carter isn't sure where it came from. If another hunter snuck in to steal her bounty, they'll be at the other end of her dagger as soon as this hellspawn is dead.

Carter rolls, reaches for her dagger again and finally snatches the hilt. Shoves the blade into the angel's chest without a second of hesitation. The steel cracks through brittle bone. She lodges her left palm against pommel to push the knife deeper and more blood spills over her fingers in spurts, hot, slippery, and steaming with sulfur, coating the gem-studded crucifix.

She grits her teeth and keeps the dagger lodged in the angel's heart until the red in its eyes dims. She's won. Somehow.

The creature goes limp and Carter lets the body fall to the side, bloody hands slipping off the hilt. As soon as she pushes the corpse away, lightning flares again, limning the silhouette of another figure.

Except this silhouette isn't human. The storm illuminates not just the figure of a woman, but also the massive feathered wings at her sides.

Carter scrambles for her weapon, yanking the blood-wet blade from her prey's chest, and holds the knife in front of her. "Don't move or you'll end up like that one."

The mysterious angel crouches down and crawls towards Carter, who skids backwards until her back hits the wall. The closer the angel creeps, the more of her features Carter can make out in the darkness. Round cheeks and dark eyes set in a smooth, bronze complexion dotted with blood spatter. Her hair gleams onyx and she has the most beautiful, full lips Carter has ever seen. Some sick compulsion urges her to reach out and brush her bloody fingers over those lips, but she keeps her hands locked on the dagger.

One thing Carter notices about the angel curdles her blood. It doesn't look fallen.

No red glow lights its eyes. No venom of sin stains its teeth or blackens those satiny white wings. This angel is straight from heaven.

Slowly, the angel reaches out and cups her hand over Carter's, still holding tight to the knife, and pushes the blade away. "I won't hurt you."

"Who are you?" Carter asks, doing her best to keep her voice steady.

The angel smiles softly, an eerie juxtaposition to the blood that spots her face like macabre freckles. "You can call me Josephine. I'm your guardian."

Oh hell no.

Carter places a bloody hand on Josephine's chest and warmth surges through her. She pushes the angel away until she falls back on her ass. "I don't need a guardian. And I don't need you getting in the way of my hunt."

Josephine purses her lips. Sure, Carter was probably a few minutes from death when Josephine showed up, but that doesn't mean Carter doesn't know what she's doing. Hunting fallen angels has been her job, her birthright, for as long as she can remember. She's never needed help before.

"I'd say you do," Josephine huffs, wings fluttering as if to enunciate her irritation. Their movement draws Carter's attention to the spotting of blood marring the immaculate feathers. "Seems like you were—"

"I wasn't in trouble." Carter tries to cover the lie by casually swiping bloodied cropped blonde hair away from her face, but only succeeds in smearing the rancid liquid across her forehead. "I would have been fine if you didn't show up. I always am."

It's never *not* been true until today. Carter has been on her own for so long, taking on the earth's most vile creatures by herself. Cleaning up after everyone else's sins. It doesn't matter that Josephine struck a violent blow to the fallen angel before Carter could finish the job. Or that Carter might actually have kicked the bucket if Josephine hadn't intervened. Shit, the angel is probably the only thing between Carter and judgment at the pearly gates right now.

Carter resents that a little. It might be a sin to take your own life, but sometimes she wishes she could be free of this fucked up family business her mother passed down to her.

Despite her exhaustion, Carter clambers to her feet, grabbing the wall for support and smearing even more blood across the peeling wallpaper. She tries to make it look graceful, but she's always been a little too bulky for that. A little too masculine.

The fallen angel. Josephine. Carter's own failure.

All of it is starting to piss her off.

"If you're my guardian"—she wipes the blade on her already ruined shirt and slides it back into its sheath at her hip—"where the fuck were you when *she* died?"

Josephine's expression cracks, and Carter gets a sickly satisfying pleasure from it. Fallen or not, angels can't be trusted. She starts to sputter an explanation, but Carter isn't interested. The memories of her mother's lifeless body on the floor of their beautiful house mute all her senses. The fallen angel standing over her, turning its crimson glare on Carter. The feeling of bloody feathers in her fists, her throat raw from screaming.

"Carter?"

She blinks back to reality, to the shitty hotel room now painted with violence, and uses the sleeve of her trench coat to wipe blood—not tears—from her cheek.

"Carter, let me help you," Josephine says from where she still sits with her back against the rickety bed.

"Help?" Carter chuckles, the sound dark but familiar in her own ears, and reaches for the cigarettes in her coat pocket. The box is squashed, nearly ruined in the scuffle, but she finds one cancer stick that isn't broken and stuffs it between her lips before feeling around her pockets for a lighter she can't seem to find. "You know I kill angels for a living, right?"

Josephine says nothing. Just stands up and raises a blood-stained hand.

Carter flinches, flushes when she realizes all Josephine was trying to do was touch the tip of the cigarette. A flame flickers at the tip and Carter inhales, only momentarily worried she's breathing in some heavenly dust worse than the chemicals and smoke she's used to. "Cute trick."

"I can do more than that." Josephine reaches out tentatively, her fingers brushing the claw wounds on Carter's neck.

The touch is so gentle. A ripple of something so much like sadness and marrow-deep want courses through Carter's veins, as if it could heal the infection of resentment rooted in her. For a second, Carter almost wants it to.

As always, the resentment wins.

Carter backs away, plucking the cigarette from her mouth. "If you're such a great guardian, you can clean up this mess by yourself," she says before she slips out the door, leaving both angels locked in the room she'll never visit again.

As she stalks the narrow hotel hall, she presses a hand to her neck and feels no wounds. No scar. Only the echo of heaven's touch.

It only takes a few days for the guardian angel to show herself again. This time, Carter's hunt goes down without a hitch. A fallen angel has been terrorizing a Catholic girls' school, and the abbess calls Carter to take care of it—probably because Carter and the abbess have had a less-than-holy relationship in the past. Carter finds the creature in one of the bathrooms, perched atop a stall, red eyes blazing in the mirror and obsidian wings extended so the scorched feathers brand ash marks into the walls.

The posturing doesn't intimidate Carter. It takes her less than a minute to finish the job.

The creature still twitches and gurgles when the pool of blood sliding along the floor splashes against Josephine's pristine white shoes. "That was easy for you."

"I told you." Carter waits for the red glow in the fallen angel's eyes to snuff out before ripping her blade out of its neck, hoping it looks casual. Like Josephine's presence hasn't caught her off guard. "I'm an expert."

"You're very competent at your profession," Josephine acknowledges, stepping away from the blood and frowning at the red stains on her shoes.

Carter finally allows her gaze to travel from Josephine's feet to her cherubic face. The light filtering in from the foggy windows gleams like a halo around her. Beautiful. Dangerous.

Carter approaches and wipes the knife on Josephine's pant leg before sliding it back into its sheath. "Then what are you doing here?"

Josephine huffs and pinches the stained fabric before giving up on it. "Something's coming." She looks around as if they're not alone. Her wings rustle gently, the only sound in the dim room aside from a broken tap dripping water into a cracked porcelain sink bowl. "I don't know when. But soon. You'll need me—*if* I decide to forgive you for ruining my clothes."

"Something is *always* coming." Carter reaches for another cigarette, this time finding her lighter before Josephine has the pleasure of *helping*. "You think you'd be able to tell by the sheer amount of fallen angels around." Cigarette between teeth, she pulls her coat around herself, fully intent on leaving this place and ditching Josephine along with the fallen angel's disintegrating body, but Josephine grabs her sleeve. Warmth runs along Carter's skin even though the angel hasn't touched her flesh. It makes Carter wish she would.

"If you won't let me help you on your jobs," Josephine says, "at least let me give you some protection."

Carter isn't sure how she does it, but Josephine suddenly has the dagger clenched in a fist and drags the blade across her palm. She hands the knife back to Carter and dips two fingers into her own blood.

Slowly, she reaches out, until her fingertips hover an inch from Carter's sweaty forehead, but Carter grabs her wrist.

Carter's heart thumps, the organ too bloated and heavy for her chest. More of that ethereal warmth drains into her from their contact point, but looking at Josephine makes her dizzy. A flood of memories demolishes her resolve and all that screams in her mind are the questions she's been longing to ask since the first time she and Josephine met.

Where were you when Mom died? Why didn't you protect us?

Carter throws Josephine's wrist aside. "I don't want your blessing."

She storms out of the school, heaving the cool morning air into her lungs, hoping it will soothe the burning in her chest. She doesn't need an angel to protect her. She doesn't need anyone.

And still, as she heads home to report the kill, all she thinks about is what it would have felt like to be touched by those divine fingertips, blessed by that celestial blood.

⸻ ❖ ⸻

Six months later, nothing has happened that would warrant Josephine's intervention. It almost makes Carter laugh every time she stabs her blade into a fallen angel and survives another kill. Not just surviving—thriving. All without the angel who said she'd need protection.

Still, the work remains brutal, life lonely. Carter often wonders, as she's finishing off her quarry, if she's really the one being punished. Her questions go unanswered. All her prayers meet silence. She's never thought much about it before, but now she can't shake the feeling that being one of the few humans in the midst of heavenly warfare should get her some kind of audience with the Big Guy. Or at least an explanation.

Winter has the city in a chokehold when Carter is called to a church, where a fallen angel has taken up residence in the rectory. Snow flurries tumble from the sky like ashes as the head priest leads Carter to the recently abandoned building. "This thing," the priest says, his breath condensing against the frigid air as if he himself breathes out brimstone, "is straight from hell. A true monster."

Despite the extra chill pulling the winter air taut, Carter smiles to herself and thumbs the pommel of her dagger. If only this man knew the real monster is her.

"I'll be praying for you," the priest says when he stops at the heavy wooden door to the ancient stone building. Of course, he won't come inside. Carter is the only one who can handle what lurks within these walls.

She pushes the door open, the iron embellishments freezing on her palm, and the hinges creak as she peeks into the dark foyer. Sulfur invades her nostrils. Evil definitely lives here.

She traverses the hallways quietly, one hand always on her holy weapon, but she finds no shadows flitting through the eerie stained-glass light. No feathers littering the stone floors. It doesn't make sense considering the dark presence that looms over the entire churchyard weighs heavier than any Carter has felt in a long time.

Carter follows the sulfur scent to a closed door at the back of the rectory. She's pretty sure this is the chapel—a private space for priests to pray. She doesn't need to go in to know this is where she will find her mark. It stinks of hell.

"Don't go in there."

She whips around, drawing her knife and pointing it at the throat of a familiar figure. The angel, Josephine, raises her hands. Probably the only human signal she knows that might convince Carter she's not a threat. The hunter knows better.

"What do you want?" Carter edges forward until the tip of her blade digs into the soft flesh under Josephine's chin.

"Just to help." The angel's wings flutter, and the rustling sends a frisson of excitement and wonder through Carter. Ever since their last encounter, she's been searching dark corners for Josephine's silken wings. Shivering every time a warm rush leaked into her in the midst of the cold. Tending to the slight stabs of disappointment when they never meet. Not that Carter really cares. But if Josephine is supposed to be her guardian, Carter would expect her to show up during missions.

Josephine's eyes flit beyond Carter to the chapel door. "There's something in there that's—"

"I know what's in there." Carter withdraws the knife but keeps it clenched in her fist. "I'm a professional, remember?" She pivots on a heel and heads for the door, ripping it open to a rusty squeal, then the silence of the chapel beyond.

"Carter!" Josephine whispers, but stays rooted to her spot in the hallway.

It's too late anyway. Carter's limbs lock as soon as she meets the pair of black eyes gaping like deep holes in the face of the creature crouched on the altar. Its claws dig into the wood, teeth drip acid onto the stone floor. The hunched body curls, haunches tucked and ready to spring as its whip-like tail knocks over the golden communion chalice.

Demon.

"Carter," Josephine whispers, somehow right in Carter's ear as goosebumps rise on the hunter's flesh so suddenly, her skin burns all over. "Do as I say."

Josephine touches her back, heat surging through her to break the demon's spell. As soon as Carter has control over her own body again, she doesn't wait for instructions. She unsheathes her knife and lunges at the beast. She's never fought a demon before, but she's studied them. Her dagger should be enough to bring down a creature like this.

Behind her, Josephine screams something, but Carter doesn't care to hear what it is.

The demon launches off the altar, an unearthly howl bellowing from its maw. Its claws meet Carter's shoulders, sinking into muscle. Carter yells in surprise and pain, but doesn't falter, even as they crash into the floor, a harsh wooden pew breaking their fall along the way.

The demon pins her to the cold stone, but Carter grips her dagger steady. She grits her teeth through the pain as she jabs it into the creature's belly.

The demon doesn't flinch. It roars and bites into Carter's throat. Hot blood floods Carter's mouth so fast she chokes on a scream. The pit-like eyes stare into her soul, trying to rip it away from her body.

So this is where it ends. Maybe she should have listened to Josephine after all. For once, Carter sort of doesn't feel like dying.

White light lances through the room. Feathers brush her cheeks and a warm tingling overcomes her as all sound fades to static. Comforting like a lover's touch. If this is what having her soul cleaved from her body feels like, Carter is lucky to have gone out this way.

———◈———

Carter gasps awake in a room lavender with dawn. Her own bedroom, her brain registers as she looks around. Her bedroom in the dingy apartment she's been renting for the past few years, walls laden with crosses and other talismans and blessings that keep hell's creatures away from her doorstep.

Her body aches. When she looks down, she finds broken skin healed over with fresh scar tissue on her chest, feels the patches of tight flesh on her neck. She's not in perfect condition, but she should be shredded demon chow. That thing tried to drag her to hell. Carter was sure it was going to succeed.

"You're awake."

In the corner of the room, Josephine is curled up in an old chair, her wings draped over the back. She looks more beautiful than ever bathed in the smoggy winter hue suffusing from the window, but Carter would never actually say that. At least, she wouldn't have before today. There's something about the way the dawn surrounds the angel that makes Carter want to touch every inch of her sanctified skin.

And there's something else…A current that buzzes between them that she's never felt before. Maybe it's the connection they've always shared, more tangible now that Josephine has touched her. That Josephine has…

Carter swallows. "You saved me, didn't you?"

Josephine nods. "It wasn't easy."

Carter almost laughs. She could have guessed that would be a tough job from the large scars across her body. "I should have listened to you."

It's hard for her to admit, but for some reason the words slip off Carter's tongue as easily as a prayer. And when Josephine comes closer, the urge to spill every sin she's ever committed rises in her throat like bile. "I should have let you help me. I shouldn't—"

Josephine reaches out to press a soft fingertip to Carter's lips. "I don't need your forgiveness, but I think there's something I should show you."

"Show me?" Carter asked, her lips brushing over Josephine's soft touch.

Josephine sits cross-legged at the end of Carter's bed and cups Carter's cheeks in her hands, warm as her palms begin to glow. Divine energy flows through them and into Carter, lighting up her veins and dissolving her consciousness from the room, from her grip on the bed sheets, even from Josephine's touch.

She blinks and she is in a place she remembers well—the beautiful old house at the end of a quiet cul-de-sac where she lived with her mother. The rattle of metal and the shattering of glass rakes through the stillness of the night. Then, a whimper.

Carter takes a few steps into the living room and peers into the shadows under the coffee table. She sees herself, eight years old, cowering. "I don't want to see this."

She waits for Josephine to pull her out of the vision, but nothing happens.

"Did you hear me?" she yells into oblivion. "I don't want to see this!"

Her apartment doesn't materialize around her. Instead, a revelation fills her to the brim and overflows and she finally understands. Josephine *needs* her to see this—for both their sakes.

"Okay." Tears bite at the corners of Carter's eyes, but she relents nonetheless. She's pushed Josephine away so many times and still the angel has shown her nothing but kindness. Josephine deserves this chance. "Into the fire."

Carter leaves her memory self and slowly walks towards the kitchen. The smashes and rattles have devolved into the wet sounds of tearing flesh. Her heart thunders when she reaches the door, cracked open. A shadow moves in the tiny sliver of light from inside. Carter knows what she will see when she goes in, and her entire body pleads for her to run, but she has to do this for Josephine. For herself.

She pushes the door open.

Blood, black in the moonlight, pools on the tile floor where her mother's body lies. Above her, a fallen angel crouches, the tips of its feathers drenched dark red, as it tears into her bowels and eats its fill. Her mother is still alive, muttering. Carter remembers her whispers as prayers to a God who didn't save her, but this time, the memory isn't quite what she recalls.

She's not praying. She's talking to someone.

Her head lies in the lap of the most beautiful angel Carter has ever seen. Feathers pristine white against bronze skin. Dark hair falls over her eyes as she cards gentle fingers through Mom's blood-matted hair, comforting her in her final moments.

Carter moves closer, carefully, as if anything she does could shatter the memory and rip away whatever she needs to gain from this. Close enough until she can make out Mom's words.

"Protect her," she says to Josephine, staring up at her with glossy eyes. "Let me die, but don't let any harm come to her. Please."

Carter doesn't need to hear Josephine's reply. She can't over the screech of the fallen angel catching sight of another victim.

She follows the evil creature's gaze to where her childhood self stands trembling in the doorway. Josephine sees her too.

The creature lunges.

The world shifts around Carter and her eyes fly open, staring directly into Josephine's. Her vision is blurry, but Josephine brushes the tears from her cheeks. "It's okay, Carter," Josephine says. "I know that was hard for you to see."

Carter didn't realize she was crying so hard. She heaves in a few deep breaths to calm herself and sunlight arcs in her veins. The same warmth she's felt on her back every time she's gone hunting. Josephine must be taking some of the pain from her, helping her. Like always.

Carter wipes her nose with the back of her arm. "You didn't save her because she asked you not to."

"She wanted me to stay with you," Josephine confirms. "So I did. I've been with you through everything. You just couldn't see me because you closed yourself off to me."

"What about the hotel?" Carter pulls back and Josephine's hands fall away from her face. The warmth flowing through her dies like a candle snuffed out by the wind. "Why did I see you there?"

A tiny smile pulls at Josephine's lips. "You hadn't really needed me until then. But in that moment, you almost died. That fallen angel would have killed you unless I intervened directly. It's not something we're supposed to do, even if someone asks us to, but..."

"But you've saved me twice recently." Carter leans forward and tips Josephine's chin up. "Even though I was a complete asshole to you. Why would you break the rules for me?"

Josephine's eyes flit down, the rising sun sparking on her lashes. Her wings shift, rustling uneasily, as if what she's about to say is difficult for her. "Because I love you, Carter."

It hits Carter then—everything she's always known but refused to believe. All that warmth, that protection that's been with her each time she risked her life...all of that was Josephine at her side.

She surges forward to take Josephine's lips with her own and the angel melts into her, as if they truly are one in the eyes of heaven. Josephine tastes sublime and feels like a perfect summer. As Carter presses the angel's back onto the blankets, the soft wings surround her. "I want to be yours," Josephine whispers as Carter kisses down her neck.

Carter wants that too. She's never bowed before God, but she lowers herself over Josephine as if prostrating before a holy altar and worships with every ounce of adoration she can muster. Her hands write prayers on the angel's skin and her mouth recites them until Josephine sings a hymn just for her. Carter gets to witness Josephine's fall from grace with her whole body and it's the most beautiful thing she's ever seen.

When they're spent, Josephine lays her head on Carter's chest. "I don't know why that's a sin," she mutters. "It's the best feeling I've ever experienced."

Carter kisses the top of her head. "I didn't know it was possible for angels to sin."

Josephine giggles, but it sounds hollow. "Where do you think fallen angels come from?"

A tiny prick of worry needles at Carter's heart. "Are you in trouble, then? You know, with the Big Man Upstairs?"

"God?" Josephine sits up, the sheets falling off her perfect, defiled body. "I don't answer to him anymore."

Carter crunches her brow. "Isn't God in charge of all the guardian angels?"

A smile pulls at Josephine's lips—a smile much less demure than the ones Carter has seen before. "I told you God doesn't like it when we intervene directly. To save you, I had to go below him."

"Below?" It's a gut wrench and a car crash and a holy dagger to the heart. Carter has spent her life fighting for heaven, because...well, because...

Josephine leans forward and takes Carter's face in her hands again. "I did say I'd do anything for you, Carter. That includes diving into hell to save your soul."

Carter gazes into Josephine's dark eyes. A hint of red flashes in her irises, but Carter doesn't feel any fear or disgust. Only love and lust and all the world's pleasure that have been denied her since she picked up her mother's mantle. "How did you do it?"

"I made a deal with Lucifer himself," Josephine says plainly. "He's not as bad as everyone says. Beautiful, actually. He said he'd spare you on the condition that we join him." She lets go of Carter and slides back on the bed so Carter can see her full form, the red scalding in her eyes, the beautiful white feathers burning black.

A fallen angel.

Carter should be disgusted. She should find her dagger and end Josephine right here on this bed, but she has no desire to do so. Only a desire for more of all that Josephine has and is.

"We?" Carter asks, hope growing roots in her for the first time since she was a child.

"Your days of chasing fallen angels are over. You'll fight for us now." Josephine takes Carter's hand and presses their palms together. Red light bursts from the connection. Heat like a brand searing into Carter's flesh and the smell of charred skin.

When Josephine removes her hand, a circle of scarlet sigils blazes on Carter's palm. Carter examines their jagged edges. She can't read them, but she knows these are evil runes. "What is this?"

"A gift," Josephine says, "in return for your services. Try it."

Carter wants to ask how but she doesn't need to. Something new courses through her blood—a dark energy that bubbles like tar and hisses like embers. She calls and it obeys without a fight. Flame bursts into her palm. It doesn't harm her, but Carter can guess it will harm anyone who gets in her way.

"Guess I'll never need you to light my cigarettes." Carter grins and meets Josephine's eyes over the eternal fire burning in the palm of her hand. Finally, she's free of the chains her mother's profession held her in. No longer a slave to a God she never wanted to serve.

Across the fire, Josephine's lips rock into a gentle smile. "Beautiful."

Carter calls up the fire in her other hand and holds death between her fingers as she gazes at the most stunning and sinful being she's ever loved. "We are."

To Sing of the Damage

Talia Greer

"I just got poison ivy up to my dick," Erik says, heaving himself onto the bus. "Fuck *me*."

The two of us who aren't currently pissing in the woods dissolve into laughter. Erik sits next to me, dripping rain, and reaches immediately for the nearest vodka bottle, but Vasya is faster.

"I didn't know we had poison ivy in this area," says Vasya. He speaks with just a slight accent, and I usually forget that he's Russian until he does something like fill his shot glass to the brim with vodka and down it all at once.

Erik waves a hand impatiently. "I dunno what it was, but it stings, and I kind of want to die."

He grabs the bottle. His face is flushed, his voice much louder than normal, and I'm already so uncomfortable I can't stand it. Everyone, except for me, has spent our entire day off drinking at the lake. And we have to work tomorrow.

"Erik, I think you've had enough," I tell him quietly.

"I'm not drinking it, Deon." He pours some vodka into his hand and slaps it into the spreading reddish blotch on his leg. There's a split second in which we all start to think his makeshift cure might actually work. Then he cries out, cursing. "Not the best of ideas."

Vasya leans outside to yell something in Russian. Jenia responds, and the forest pissing party ends. She takes a seat near the front of the bus, across from our camp director Marina Paulovna, who's been sound asleep the entire ride back from the lake.

"We have medical assistance at camp, Erik," Vasya says. "Jenia will take you when we return."

Erik puts on an ominous voice. "If we ever return."

All of us follow his gaze. The view from the window is almost completely obscured by a dense sheet of rain. *I* can't see the road from where I'm at, so I can't imagine how the camp bus driver can, either. At first I think that's why we aren't moving.

"You are correct," Jenia ventures in English. She hesitates, then abandons the attempt and adds something else in her native tongue.

Vasya chuckles. "She says it is raining so much, and there is so much water, we may drown when simply standing out-side. The other *vozhati* we await should hurry her journey."

"What counselor?" I ask. "Are we picking someone up?"

"Is that her?"

Erik points out the window. A barelyvisible figure approach-es through the downpour, carrying a bag at her side. When the bus door opens, I tense. I haven't been at ease around water for a long time, and seeing how much this girl has obviously dealt with it unsettles me.

She's incredibly thin, with long, pale blonde hair soaked by the rain. Her clothes—a simple blue summer dress—are wet as well. A puddle seems to follow her as she navigates to the back of the bus and sits on a bench to the right of Erik and I. She introduces herself in Russian and continues on, and I give Vasya a look. He grins, saying something to her, and I think he's telling her we're Americans.

"Oi!" The girl from the rain turns to us, smiling. "I am Anastasia Valerovna. But please call me Nastia."

Erik shakes her hand. "I'm Erik, and this is my roommate Deon."

There's that lurch in my stomach. The guilty stab of hiding the truth. Erik is my boyfriend, but we don't tell people that until we know they're safe—my very existence as a black dude out here is already scandalous enough—and we certainly don't go broadcasting it around camp. This new girl is an entirely unknown entity. Of course, we're not telling her anything.

I nod at her in greeting and look quickly away. It's raining harder now, and internally, I am screaming at the bus to move.

"We're volunteering this summer for college credit," Erik adds. When I don't offer anything up, he continues. "Deon's not normally this quiet, but water freaks him out. He can barely handle taking showers."

"Erik–"

"What? It's true."

I swallow my words. He's drunk. Telling him he's bothering me is pointless.

Erik gives me a look that I know means *I'm sorry*, and my anger melts somewhat. Part of me is pleased that he still knows me so well, even when he's drunk, even when we're so far from home. Discreetly, between our legs on the bus bench, I lace our fingers together. He squeezes my hand. Something about his presence calms my anxiety about the worsening storm, and I feel myself relax.

Nastia absorbs the exchange with a small, calculating smile on her face. I really wish she wouldn't.

⸺⸻◈⸻⸺

The knock comes at exactly seven-thirty, as always.

"*Dobre ootra!*" someone calls from the hallway. *Good morning!*

I've already been awake for an hour, watching Erik across the room to make sure he was still breathing. I've never seen him drink so much. He said he was fine, but I had to be sure. I watch for one final time the slow rise and fall of his chest beneath the covers. I watch the chunk of coppery hair over his eye that moves ever so slightly when he exhales. Between each breath, there's a brief moment of panic in which I worry another won't follow. I'm so wound up, I'm surprised I even slept. But when I sit up, I have to shake off fatigue all the same.

"Erik." I slowly get out of bed, making as much noise as possible. I grab shower gel and a towel and loudly clear my throat. "Time to get up."

"*Ya ni hachu,*" he whines. *I don't want to.*

"Don't try to distract me by using bits of Russian you've picked up because you know I think it's cute. If you're not up when I get out of the shower, I'm coming in there after you."

Erik grins, eyes still closed. "All right."

I didn't mean it like *that,* but I'm already too flustered to explain, so I just leave.

When I get back, he's up and dressed, knotting his shoelaces. I return my shower supplies to their proper place and find some clothes.

"So what exactly happened last night? Because I'm pretty sure I blacked out sometime during the walk back up the hill from the lake."

I whirl around in a panic. *Was he really that drunk?*

Erik laughs. "Dude, *relax.* That was a joke."

I face the wall again to put my shirt on.

"It wasn't funny."

"I remember everything, I swear." Suddenly I feel him behind me, his arms around my waist. His chin on my shoulder. He's warm and smells like sleep, and I melt into his touch. "I'm sorry, okay?"

I sigh. "No, *I'm* sorry. I'm being an idiot. I'm just...not handling the rain well." *And I'm not used to having to hide, not like this.* "But I know that's not an excuse."

"It definitely is." He kisses my cheek, and I hear him move toward the door. "Now, I either need to eat or throw up, so I'm gonna head to breakfast and figure out which one it is."

I turn as he leaves. As I'm grabbing my keys so I can follow him, something on his bed catches my eye. A small circle near his pillow is a darker blue than the rest of the sheets. Wet, it seems, but I'm not sure with what.

My chest tightens. If our room has a leak, and rain has seeped in from a crack in the window, I think I will actually come fully unglued. I tell myself it's drool, or sweat, so I won't worry about another possibility. Then I run to breakfast.

The cafeteria is half empty, most of the older groups of children not yet arrived. My assigned *otryad*—a group of twelve campers, ages six to eight—appears to already have eaten quite a bit, which gives me only a few minutes before I have to leave with them. I hurry to one of the staff tables, where Jenia and Vasya are sitting, and start shoving kasha and eggs down my throat. The oatmeal-like texture of the kasha isn't fun at high speeds, but I've got no other choice.

"Are you well, Deon?" asks Vasya.

I nod. "Trying to eat before my group leaves."

"Ah."

"Vassily Leonidovich?" Both of us turn toward the sound of his name. Marina Paulovna appears and quickly relays some information. Behind her is Nastia, who smirks at me. She's dressed in the camp-issued white polo with gold lettering, along with a pair of dark jeans. With her hair in a high ponytail, she looks every bit a counselor like the rest of us, but it fails to set me at ease.

"Nastia will be working with Erik and I now," Vasya summarizes.

"Oh."

Strange. Each group is usually assigned only two counselors, who look after them and lead them around to activities all day. I guess Nastia's arrival has thrown off the numbers.

Nastia steps forward. "Yes, I am very happy. We will have much fun together."

I try to generate a response, but I can't get past the look in her eyes. How desperate she seems. For what, though? Why does everything about this girl give me such bad vibes?

Vasya stretches up on his tiptoes, scanning over the top of campers' heads. "Have you seen Erik?"

I point across the room to where Erik sits with his table of campers. The ends of two spoons stick down out of his mouth on either side like silver tusks, making him look like a giant ginger walrus. His campers roar with laughter.

Vasya and Nastia head in that direction just as I see Jenia signal our group to leave. I follow her and our campers past the dish drop-off and toward the door. When I turn to make sure we've got all our kids, my eyes go instead back to Erik, his head now thrown back in laughter, the spoons clattering to the table, and Nastia chuckling quietly across from him.

Craft hour. Sticky hands. Shrieking giggles. Soccer games. The morning blurs into afternoon, and before I know it, lunch is over. Returning to my room afterward is tricky: my shoes leak mud from the rain-soaked soccer field. Somewhere, the cleaning staff is cursing me into the depths of the Moscow septic system.

But next is rest hour, and Erik and I swore early on that this would be our daily time together. We're each so busy during the school year that we hardly see each other. This volunteer study abroad trip was supposed to be our attempt at creating some time for *us*. And since we've been pretending to be just friends to the camp administration, this time is even more important. It's a cruel irony that we're busier here, enough to have to schedule dates.

I slip my shoes off as I cross the threshold, then sit on the bed. From two floors below, there's the faint scream of a young camper being particularly uncooperative about naptime. And then from the hallway, footsteps.

In rushes Erik. I've just opened my mouth to speak when I realize he's moving at the speed of light with no apparent intention of stopping.

"Erik?"

"I just came to drop off my stuff." He rips open his backpack's zipper and snatches out a package of markers, each of them thick as a cigar. "I have to go help Nastia work on a poster for the acting competition tonight."

For a moment, I just look at him. He keeps moving, finds a pair of scissors, adds them to the markers. He doesn't seem to notice anything wrong.

"I'll see you later, okay?" Erik grabs some Scotch tape and holds everything against his chest.

"Erik—"

But he's gone.

I sit stunned. Embarrassment washes over me in waves so hot I know I'd be red if my skin weren't so dark. I don't understand—did I do something? Something so awful he'd blow me off without any real explanation? We've been together for years—he could at least tell me if I've done something wrong.

I can't stand sitting around and being upset. So I decide to go for a walk.

Here, the outdoors has become my respite, never failing to calm my mounting anxiety. The air is fresh and energizing with a crispy sort of summer heat, the sky a perfect endless blue. Trees stretch up and on for ages, and between them, off in the distance, lies the vastness of the glittering lake.

I follow the lake path until I reach the beach, then slip off my sandals and shuffle through the sand. I walk the beach in one direction as far as we're allowed, and when I turn back, I notice people at the opposite end, near the dock.

A closer inspection reveals Erik and Nastia. They sit near the water, both leaning over a large poster.

There's a stab of pain in my chest as I watch Nastia pause, marker in hand, and gesture towards the lake. She says something to Erik that I can't make out from a distance, but she soon strips down to a bathing suit and wades into the water.

From my hiding spot behind a tree, I glue my narrowed eyes to Erik. Counselors aren't supposed to swim unless they're off the clock, late at night.

And don't they have a poster to make?

I grip the bark to steady myself as he lays aside his scissors and moves to join Nastia.

My anxiety peaks, and I tell myself it's just because of my proximity to the water, but I know it's not. I fume all the way back to the room and stare at the ceiling until snack time.

For today's snack, the cafeteria serves up kisel, a thick fruit drink, served hot. It's bright pink from the red currants that form its base. The texture is how I imagine warm Jell-O might feel. It's by far the strangest thing I've eaten here, but it's grown on me, becoming a small comfort. Today, though, I can only manage a sip or two before feeling nauseous. I reach for an energy bar instead.

Erik slides into a seat across from me with wet hair and a smile. The energy bar in my hand caves to the slight pressure of my fist.

"Woah," he says, catching sight of my face. "Who peed in your kasha?"

I take care to appear normal. I don't respond.

"That lake is *beautiful*, Deon. I know you don't like water, but I wish you'd at least walk over there with me sometime. I think you'd enjoy it."

There's a bad taste in my mouth as I bite back the words, *I was just there. Watching you. With Nastia.*

Instead I grit out, "How's that new counselor in your group?"

Erik frowns. "Nastia? What about her?"

"I dunno. It's weird to gain a new co-counselor in the middle of the session."

A corner of Erik's mouth twitches up. "Are you jealous?"

"Why the hell would I be jealous?"

"You're wearing the same face you did when I won Prom King in high school and had to dance with Allie Ryan for a whopping three minutes."

I roll my eyes. He might be right, but I'm not going to admit it. Erik laughs and drains the last of his water.

"Trust me." He squeezes my hand, briefly. "There's nothing to worry about."

———◈———

Several days pass, each fraught with similar disappointments. I exhaust myself planning activities for my group and Jenia starts to worry. One night before dinner, she takes me aside and essentially forces me to take an unofficial night off. I don't have a choice.

I stop by the camp store to pick up some packaged noodles for dinner. I'm almost looking forward to an early night. Sleep has become my only escape from Erik's nonsense, and I'm ready to welcome it as an old friend.

The first thing immediately obvious upon entering our room is the reek of damp fabric. Erik's bed is soaked. Not like the result of an open window during a storm, but *deliberately* wet, like someone intended to play a prank and dumped buckets upon buckets of water here.

Anxiety claws at my throat. Usually, Erik waits for me and we walk over to dinner together.

If he's not here...

I poke my head into the hallway. Maybe he's running late returning from his group duties. It's then that I hear the shower running. The relief is staggering. I sprint toward the bathroom at the end of the hall, instantly more excited than I've been in a week.

My shoes lose traction just inside the bathroom doorway, and I quickly brace myself on a sink for balance. Water covers the entire floor, seeping out from the shower stalls. There's enough to make me think every shower and faucet in the room is turned on full blast, but only one of the stalls is closed, and none of the sinks are running.

Slowly, I stand up. Chills race up and down my skin, and my heartbeat kicks into overdrive.

The water was over my head, a deep, impenetrable black. I couldn't see the boat anymore. Couldn't hear Mom screaming for me, though I knew she was. I thrashed frantically, searching for the surface, but I no longer knew which way was up, and water rushed into my nose—my lungs—couldn't breathe, couldn't breathe—

"Deon?"

Erik stands before me, dressed and rubbing a towel through his hair. The water is gone.

Slowly, he says, "What are you doing?"

"N-Nothing."

I'm trembling. How long have I been standing here? I have to bring myself back. Bathroom, not lake. I'm twenty-one in a communal bathroom at a Russian summer camp, not near-drowning in a lake at age ten. There is no threat. *Relax.*

"Looking for you," I add.

"I was just taking a shower..."

I can see the pity approaching. I don't want it.

"Your bed was wet," I tell him.

"What?"

"Soaked, Erik. Like someone dumped water on it."

He's frowning. Shaking his head. "It was probably just the light."

"I don't think–"

"Listen, I've got to go."

My stomach lurches. "Go *where*?"

"I'm actually going out with Nastia and some of the other counselors. Apparently there's a great restaurant right on the edge of town that they go to all the time." He drapes the towel over his shoulder and glances at himself in the mirror. "I'm late already."

I wait for him to invite me.

He doesn't.

"Come on, Deon." His voice softens. "Don't look at me like that."

"I'm not looking at you any specific way," I say, wounded.

"It's not my fault you haven't made any friends," he says.

The look on my face must be response enough. He grimaces in pained apology and leaves without another word.

Don't leave me, I want to yell at him. *Please.*

Instead, I force my legs to move. Then they take charge, carrying me out of the bathroom, down the hall, and into the other wing of the staff floor. I move with purpose until I'm standing in Vasya's open doorway. He told us once we could stop by and hang out anytime, and I intend to take him up on the offer tonight.

"Deon!" Jenia gets up off the couch to hug me. She pulls me down next to her and points at the soccer game on TV, and then proceeds to give me what I assume is a recap. I nod even though I don't understand.

Vasya returns a moment later with a plate of hastily-arranged sandwiches and a tall, thin bottle of vodka. Jenia starts babbling about me to him and I sit and stare blankly.

"Are you well, Deon?"

I nod. As he moves past me to the small table, I take some of the vodka off his hands and drink straight from the bottle. Jenia gasps.

"I thought you did not drink," says Vasya, wide-eyed.

"I do now."

He makes no further comment.

———◈———

When I wake up, I'm being violently shaken, and Jenia's face looms above.

"Wake, Deon! Wake!"

I can hardly speak, she's moving me so much. Her hands grasp my shoulders almost to the point of bruising.

"Jenia–*Jenia!* I'm up!"

She ceases the unexpected thrashing and rattles off some rapid fire Russian, of which I understand, "Marina Paulov-na—you must—to—breakfast—come!"

She hurries off, leaving me with an awful thrashing pain in my skull I didn't notice before. Am I hungover?

My stomach roils, and I have no choice but to run for the bathroom.

I stare at the contents of my stomach as they leave my body and try to remember what happened last night. Unsurprisingly, there's nothing. All I know is I drank vodka until the memory of the way Erik looked at me in the bathroom stopped hurting as much. Until my own paranoia and insecurities faded into a warm fuzz in my chest, and the soccer game on TV blurred entirely sideways.

When I stop puking, I stick my head in the shower, dry off, and head down to breakfast as quickly as possible.

There's a significant bubble of tension surrounding the staff table that thickens when I arrive. Marina Paulovna barely spares me a glance before she returns to speaking furiously at the other counselors. I pick a spot on the table and stare until it's over and I can find Vasya to translate.

Afterwards, he speaks quietly to me. "Late yesterday evening, a bathroom in our building was flooded, and there are rumors—" Vasya breathes deeply. "There are rumors of *vozhati*...misbehaving in a shower stall."

"Which counselors?" I ask, though something about his tone is already confirming my suspicions.

"Anastasia Valerovna—Nastia. And—And Erik."

I feel like I've just been punched in the face. What the *fuck* were Nastia and Erik doing in a flooded shower stall together?

Why won't he talk to me anymore?

Why has everything gone to shit since *she* arrived?

"I am sorry, Deon," Vasya says gently. "Perhaps you should speak with Erik—"

Something inside me switches off, and I storm off. The next thing I'm aware of is charging toward the room, unsteady with anger. I shove the door open so hard it ricochets off the wall. In the rush of the early morning, I didn't even think about Erik.

Now I can't believe I didn't notice he was there, still in bed, curled up facing the wall.

"Erik!"

This time, I don't wait for him to respond. I seize his shoulder and yank so he's facing me.

And everything stops.

He's drenched, his entire body much colder than normal. Small patches of sand fall off his skin when I start to shake him, like Jenia previously shook me. His lips are bluish. He reeks of lake water.

He's not breathing.

"Erik!"

My camp-required CPR training kicks in. I start chest compressions, screaming all the while until someone appears.

I don't breathe until he does. I don't breathe until he leans over and vomits water onto the floor, until he succumbs to coughing so forceful it likely won't ever stop.

The aftermath is a blur. The camp nurses fussing over Erik, wondering why he can't remember what happened. Vasya and Jenia hovering in an attempt to be helpful.

Nastia, strangely absent.

And me, fleeing outside, trying to escape before my head explodes.

Erik is fine, he will be fine. But he almost wasn't. As the adrenaline of the emergency ebbs away, I'm left shaky and cold, and above all, angry.

I find myself wandering the camp grounds. The lake looms ahead, and I start to make a conscious effort to avoid it in favor of a more wooded trail. Then I notice movement: in the corner of a tree branch several feet from the ground, a pale leg shifts positions.

Nastia waves as I approach, all friendly, like she's been waiting all along. Dressed in her blue summer dress again, she's draped herself over a branch, her back to the tree trunk, and runs a delicate golden comb through the near-translucent strands of her hair.

"You will go to swim, Deon?" she asks, gesturing to the lake with the comb.

"No," I spit out. "I will not."

She gathers her hair over one shoulder. It cascades down into her lap, almost as if it has a mind of its own.

"But the water, it is lovely."

I don't know who or what she is, but I do know that Erik hasn't been himself since she arrived. A shout erupts from my throat, surprising even myself.

"What did you do to Erik?" I yell.

Nastia recoils as if I've slapped her. "I have done nothing. What is wrong?"

"Is it drugs?" I demand, desperate possibilities racing through my mind. "Some sort of freaky Russian meth?"

"Deon, I do not–"

"Look, you stupid bitch, something happened to him once you two started spending time together. And I *don't* like it. So either you tell me what the fuck is going on or I make up some excuse to get Erik and I sent home."

Nastia regards me calmly. She's silent for so long I don't know if she'll ever actually speak. As she shakes her hair so it falls down her back, she says, "Do what you like. Erik's faith for me is strong. He will not leave."

"What the hell does that mean?"

She smiles that infuriating smile once more, and turns away, resuming her hair maintenance.

The longer I spend in her presence, the more I feel like screaming and screaming until my throat goes raw. But that won't get me answers.

So I swallow everything I feel, and force myself back inside to check on Erik.

———◈———

I don't sleep that night.

Instead, I lie awake, staring at the ceiling, and strain my ears for the sound of Erik's breath. I turn Nastia's words over in my mind—*Erik's faith for me is strong*—and grasp for meanings to unpack. Around me, the night stretches on, silent and unyielding.

I must doze off at some point, because I open my eyes to the creaking of Erik's bed. He rolls over to touch his feet to the floor and rises in one fluid motion. Then, slowly, he steps out into the hallway. Fighting through waves of fatigue, I get up and follow him.

"Erik?" I whisper.

He walks with purpose, but doesn't respond.

I quicken my pace. The camp at night is an eerie place. Darkened buildings bathe in moonlight, cushioned by green-black foliage. Out of all the shapes looming in the darkness, I follow the one that moves, down the path to the lake.

As soon as my feet touch the sand, it's as if the air's been vacuumed from my lungs. Erik continues moving and inching ever closer to the water. I'm frozen at the sand's edge.

"Erik, *please*. What are you doing?"

One distant lamppost from the boat corral illuminates his face as he looks to his left.

Then: "Nastia?" he calls out.

My heart stops. Somehow, she was right. She's stolen him from me, so fast I didn't even realize I'd lost him.

At the edge of the water, Erik hesitates. Calls for her once more. And proceeds to move deeper.

The surge comes out of nowhere. Water rents itself apart with a great burst and collapses upon Erik. There's a brief and violent thrashing of waves before he's swallowed by the darkness, and all at once, the lake is still.

Panic breaks my hesitation. I run headlong at the water, tearing into the shallow end with everything I've got. Instant chill bumps raise on my skin as for a moment, I'm blinded by the cold and the fear. I don't want to move. The cold seeps into my bones, freezing me from the inside out.

But *Erik*.

I begin the process of moving my right leg forward.

And the water explodes once again, this time launching at me a bony, white figure. The force knocks me onto my back. Water rushes into my mouth and nose and I cough and sputter and crawl backwards, crablike, grasping for dry sand, for anything—

Hands slam my shoulders into the ground. Knotted strands of green-blue hair form a curtain around my head. Thin but powerful legs straddle my torso.

Nastia smiles down at me, her mouth full of teeth three times too many. Black fills the whites of her eyes. She's naked, the skin of her torso pale and translucent. Through it, I glimpse her ribcage, her beating heart.

She breathes a deep, rattling breath.

"Deon," she says. "You stupid, stupid boy."

I lie absolutely still. I'm convinced that none of this is real, that it can be wished away in an instant with just the right amount of determination.

Nastia releases one of my shoulders to run a skeletonlike hand along my jaw, whispering, "You should have just stayed away."

She's right. "Where's Erik?" I demand.

"He is *mine.* My prize. No longer yours."

I crane my head to look past her and she slams me down hard enough to momentarily blacken my vision.

"I can make you hurt," she tells me. "Hurt like you did that day on the boat."

Her strength is unnatural, and she shouldn't know about the boat. None of this is right. We *have* to get away from her.

"How did you know that?" I ask. Maybe she'll elaborate. Buy me some time to fight my growing headache, gain the upper hand.

"Shhh," says Nastia, gentle like soothing a cranky camper to sleep.

A flick of her wrist, and she pulls the water up and over my head. But only briefly.

Being submerged like this should send me into a tailspin. It doesn't. Instead, the thought of Erik sharpens my focus. When I can breathe again, I rear up against her. I struggle and scream for Erik and try to spot him, but I can't, no matter how hard I try.

"Where is he?"

"He is mine," she repeats.

Some distance away, the water bubbles.

Despair overwhelms me. He's underwater, and I can't get to him.

Sobbing, I lie still. "Please," I beg. "Just let him go."

Nastia slowly shakes her head. I picture Erik under the surface, confident in his swimming skills until the moment he realizes they're nowhere near enough. I picture him sucking in pure water, suffocating on it.

"Please!" I scream. "Just–just–"

I don't know what I'm asking. I just can't imagine him being gone.

Her head tilts to the side. "Yes?"

I swallow. And it hits me all of a sudden. A compromise that might interest her.

"Take me instead."

The words are shaky, but my intent is strong. I'll do anything to save Erik. He's all I have. But I'm *not* all that he has. He's so much more vibrant and full of life. If either of us deserves to walk away from this, it's him.

Nastia goes still. She blinks, showering me with a sprinkle of wet sand.

"Interesting," she says, the word oozing like poison sludge. Her smile widens, on and on, until every tooth is showing.

There is no deliberation. No lengthy preface. One moment is all it takes for the water to close over my head.

Dad was supposed to be watching me. He was supposed to help me reel in whatever fish I caught. But when my catch toppled my balance and pulled me over, he was too preoccupied with his beer.

I kick to the surface for one blessed moment. And my eyes go to Erik, slumped in a heap on the beach.

I didn't know how to swim yet. So when the water closed in, I panicked. I took a breath. But that time, someone was there to pull me out.

He's not moving. For a single terrifying second, I'm not sure he will. I'm underwater again before I can find out.

Then I hear it.

"Deon?"

He's confused. He doesn't get it. But Nastia bats me around a bit, gifting me with one brief glimpse of the grey-black sky, and then he does.

"*Deon!*" he roars.

His voice is muffled from underwater, but the message is all the same. I see him in my mind looking hurt and wondering above all else why I'm leaving him, when it really couldn't be farther from the truth.

Nastia's skeletal limbs entwine with mine, dragging me down. My fear is neutralized by the cold and by the acceptance of this reality as the only available option.

Before the dark, there is but the look on Erik's face, and imminent glow of teeth moving ever closer. There's nothing I can do. I know what's coming.

I go limp and wait for death.

Then a strong hand closes around my bicep, and suddenly I'm being dragged from the water, ripped from Nastia's grasp, through the shallows and into the sand. The person is grumbling, cursing a mile a minute. Harsh blows rain down on my chest.

"*Breathe!*"

Vasya. I cough up water into his face. Satisfied, he tears himself away, out of view.

He saved me. But where's Erik?

With a weak hand, I wipe water from my eyes, and find Erik on his knees among the waves lapping at the shore. With Vasya's help, he has Nastia pinned down.

She looks somehow more unnatural now, her limbs more elongated, her many rows of teeth sharper and longer in the moonlight.

"You can't have him," snarls Erik.

Unconcerned, Nastia lets out a high, eerie peal of laughter.

"And who are you to stop me?"

Erik and Vasya, both of them, they're too close to her. Not safe. I force myself up and moving. As I do, something falls from my shirt, ice cold and glinting gold in the moonlight.

Nastia's comb.

In my hands, it's sturdier than it looked before. Metal, not plastic. It must have gotten entangled in my clothes when she tried to kill me.

And I am not above using it to defend myself against her.

I crawl towards them as fast as I can, the comb gripped tightly in my hand.

Nastia roars with otherworldly laughter. She bucks and thrashes, the two of them seeming to only barely keep her contained. "I am of the sea. You cannot kill me!"

Erik and Vasya hesitate. Whether that's true or not, I don't intend to find out. I reach deep for the last of my energy and toss myself into the fray.

"Deon, no!" Erik shouts.

I land on top of Nastia. My hands fumble on the comb before finding grip. I anchor my elbows against her chest, pushing with both hands, and shove the comb into her throat just below her chin.

She gurgles, thrashing out, but Erik keeps her held down. Vasya leverages his entire weight against the comb. It sinks into her skin until all I see is the gilded edge, and the sickly blue-green blood that wells up beneath it. Once, twice more she thrashes, before going still.

For a moment there is only the sound of the lake lapping against the shore. Then, with a noise like a sudden downpour, Nastia's body begins to shimmer. In seconds it's gone, dissolved into nothing, leaving us clutching handfuls of wet sand.

Erik lets out a huff and sits back on his heels. Vasya stands and looks out across the lake, his expression a slash of cautious disgust. Finally, he crosses himself, spits three times over his left shoulder, and says, "Be gone, rusalka."

I'm gasping, on the verge of a complete meltdown, but I need to know. "How did you know?"

"I didn't," says Vasya. "Not until tonight."

A shiver steals over me then, and I give in. I curl up on the sand with exhaustion chattering my bones. Erik's arms slip beneath me and pull me to him. We're both soaked, we nearly died, but we're here and *alive* and I am so, so grateful for that.

He cradles my head in his lap. I start sobbing.

"Don't worry," Erik says, shushing me. *My* Erik. He never left me after all. "I've got you."

Sceadugenga

Ben Marit

CONTENT WARNINGS: DESCRIPTIONS OF OFF-SCREEN VIOLENCE

BEOWULF, young hero of the Geats, blessed of the Lord, strong of mind and body, his legend growing by the day, was...conflicted.

Heorot, the great mead hall of the Danes, was in shambles. The terrifying claw-arm of the devil Grendel lay bloody and grotesque on the reddened wood underfoot. Beowulf's companions and the native Scyldings of King Hroðgar, the latter pouring in from where they had been sleeping, crowded around the hall.

All but Hondscio, that was.

Grendel had fallen on him first, bursting through the great doors and attacking with single-minded ferocity. Hondscio had died on his feet with a cry of defiance in his throat. A warrior's death.

Beowulf regretted the loss of his friend but pushed the grief from his mind when King Hroðgar entered the hall. The fidgety man, bedecked in robes and jewels, a never-used sword at his hip, stared around in wonder before landing on Beowulf.

"You have done it," he said, arms spreading wide. "You have freed my hall from the terror of that creature."

Then folk produced casks of mead, a feast was prepared, and a scop began the celebrations with a song.

But still, Beowulf was conflicted.

Grendel's claw-arm, tacked to the wall above the hearth as a trophy for the king of the Scyldings, drew his gaze.

The devil's face returned to his mind, eyes burning red with anger, rage, and barely concealed panic at his unforeseen opponent. For the first time in twelve years, the devil had met his match and saw death. His mouth opened, guttural words low for Beowulf's ears alone.

"The murderer king has lost the stomach for his own evil? Had to find some foreign stripling to do it instead?"

Beowulf tore Grendel's arm from its socket and secured his greatest victory yet.

He blinked away the image, but the word remained.

Murderer.

He pulled his attention from the grisly prize to Hroðgar at the high table, his meek, silent wife shrinking from his boisterous drunkenness. The king sloshed mead from his horn, threw a bawdy jest at one of Beowulf's remaining thirteen. Hamo returned a laugh, but the smile didn't reach his eyes.

Beowulf clenched his jaw and sat back, letting the jibes and merriment flow around him. The mead turned to acid in his mouth. Hay had been thrown about to soak up the blood, but the pungent tinge of violence still choked his nostrils.

He couldn't trust an agent of the Enemy. He was Beowulf, thane and hero, not some monk set to ponder the idle words of a devil.

And yet he pondered.

Hroðgar leaned to his lady wife and whispered something into her ear. The color drained from her face. Her spine straightened and her jaw flexed, face toward the far wall. She said something Beowulf couldn't make out and her husband growled, brows furrowing over beady eyes. His body tensed and his lady wife shrank in reflex, but the king took a breath, glanced around the crowded hall. His gaze met Beowulf's, and he forced a grin, lifting his cup in Beowulf's direction.

Beowulf did not return the gesture.

⸻⬤⸻

Later, he stepped into the frosty night, glad to be free of the stifling heat.

"You aren't enjoying the celebration?" Aelfric asked from a stool near the hall.

Beowulf approached, watching the cold stars overhead. "I find myself in a glum mood tonight, my friend."

Aelfric cocked his head. "This is a glorious victory. Should you not be proud of your deeds? We are."

Beowulf had no answer. The darkness of the far coastline drew his gaze.

Aelfric's eyes followed. "The sentries say the devil fled towards the mere on the far hills. They say that is where the monster comes from."

Beowulf nodded slowly, then squared his shoulders, flexed his neck. "I will return by tomorrow eve." He stepped from the light of the hall towards the encroaching dark.

Aelfric gasped and rushed after him. "Beowulf! The devil is surely dead from the grievous wound you delivered. Don't you think collecting its head can wait 'til morning?"

"I must be sure," Beowulf lied over his shoulder.

Picking up the devil's trail was simple, even in the dark. Black blood dotted the trails and undergrowth, still bubbling even after hours in the cold.

As Beowulf approached the dark mere his worry grew. What, exactly, was he doing here? He couldn't rightly say, only that some inner instinct was prickling at his mind, urging him onwards. Aelfric was almost certainly right—the devil would be dead by now. Nothing, not even a servant of the Enemy, could survive without an arm for long. But the devil's words...

The water was glass smooth, utterly black, standing out against the moonless night. A tuft of bramble took up the far shore, dribbles of blood leading in that direction. Beowulf followed until the trail disappeared into the water. This did not concern him: he had slain creatures of the deep before, thrashing and slashing in the depths, only to come out more the hero in his homeland. So, throwing off his mail coat and tossing his sword aside—the devil was impervious to its blade, a fell blessing of the Enemy—he jumped in. The water was bitingly cold, but that was no matter. Using his hands, he navigated the utter black to find a tunnel in the lakebed. It tracked for some yards before ascending once more, spitting him out into a gloomy chamber, stale but breathable air filling his lungs.

No sounds of alarm met his ears, no sense of movement but the drip-drop of water from his own clothing. However, a faint, eerie blue light emanated from the far end of the natural tunnel. He paced it with slow, deliberate steps, senses alert.

A second, larger chamber opened around him. Brackish pools dotted its floor, stalactites reaching down from the ceiling, and still the glow lit the space. He searched for the source but found none—it came from everywhere and nowhere. Surely the magic of the Enemy at play.

Motion or something akin to it drew him to attention. His muscles flexed of their own accord, a lifetime of conflict drilled into them.

He was being watched.

"Sceadugenga!" he said, taking a step forward, raising his chin. "Come forth and answer for your deeds."

A long silence followed before a darkened silhouette appeared in a far shadow.

"You call me thus, and yet you are the one skulking about," a rough voice came. It was the devil, but the guttural quality from before was absent.

"Come into the light or I will drag you."

Another moment of hesitation before the devil complied.

Beowulf inhaled sharply.

Before him was no devil of claw and shadow, of burning eyes and terrible rage. No, a man stepped into the ambient light, tired and haggard. A light beard shaped his face. He wore a simple, threadbare tunic and doeskin breeches, bare feet on the cold stone.

And he had both arms. He cradled his right arm gently with the other and winced at the movement, but it was whole and intact.

Sunken, dark eyes found Beowulf's.

"Why have you come here, thrall of Hroðgar? To gloat? To finish your master's task?"

Beowulf opened his mouth to boast but found no words.

Why *had* he come here? For a moment, he forgot.

Beowulf cleared his throat. "I come of my own will, devil." The bravado leeched from his voice and he swallowed. "Though I did not expect..."

The man tilted a brow. "Did not expect what, sword-slave of Heorot? A man like yourself?"

"What are you?" Beowulf demanded.

"I am Grendel," the man said with a scoff. "Or so your master calls me. A devil, a *gaest*, the nightmare of the Scyldings." He shrugged. "Isn't it obvious?"

"You were different. Earlier."

Grendel nodded. "I was. And I will be again."

"How?"

"You are curious for a hired sword."

Beowulf stood to his full height, chest out, though he noticed with some discomfort that the man opposite him was equally tall, even stooped as he was. "I am Beowulf, sworn thane of King Hygelac of Geatland. My father owed King Hroðgar a debt, and so I am here to repay it."

"By killing me?"

"By putting a stop to your butchery."

Grendel barked a coarse, mirthless laugh. "*Butchery*. You call me butcher?"

"Scores of Danes have you murdered and devoured, and —"

"And scores more will I," Grendel said sharply. "Hroðgar has earned it all and more."

Beowulf examined the man, his purpose in coming here bubbling to his tongue. "*Murderer*, you called him when we battled. What did you mean?"

Grendel was silent for a long time, expression suspicious. "You do not know?"

"Would I ask if I did?" Beowulf snapped. "Tell me or I will finish my task."

Grendel huffed. "Threats do not befit you, thane of Hygelac. We both know now I cannot win, even with the blessing of Woden upon me. If it is your vile trade you seek to practice tonight, then practice and be done with it."

Beowulf clenched his fists, patience ebbing, but he bit back a retort and kept his footing. He leveled his voice with some effort. "What did you mean by *murderer*?"

"You truly wish to know?"

Beowulf gave a sharp nod.

Grendel watched him for another long moment. Beowulf could feel the calculation, the inner conflict, but finally Grendel sighed, his shoulders dropping. "Follow me." Without waiting for a response, he turned and melded into the deep shadows.

Beowulf hesitated. Could this be a trick? A ruse of the Enemy, intent on dropping Beowulf's guard?

But no. As Grendel had said, they both knew Beowulf was the better fighter now. Even in these cramped confines, he would be victorious. So, he followed, a tunnel revealing itself. It veered off sharply into the hills, utterly silent but for the soft pad of his feet on stone and the thrum of blood in his ears.

The tunnel opened, and...

Beowulf stumbled to a halt, his breath catching.

This second chamber was massive, expanding deep into darkness, ceiling hidden in the gloom. Small hovels dotted the space, though many appeared abandoned, dilapidated, holes worn in their hide coverings. Heads peeked at him from around corners, wide, scared faces finding him in Grendel's wake. Grendel stopped and peered about before turning to Beowulf.

He was close now, only a few feet separating them. His eyes were dark even in the expanded light of this chamber. A scar ran from his forehead to his chin, cutting a path through his short beard. His hair was shaggy and matted with the water of the mere. His arm, which Hroðgar currently had pinned upon the hearth in Heorot, was mottled and gray as if dead.

Grendel's gaze met his, and Beowulf could not stop the stutter in his breast. He cleared his throat and looked away. "What is this place?"

"The last redoubt of my people," Grendel said simply. "The object of Hroðgar's bloodlust."

Beowulf's shoulders slumped and his brow furrowed. "What did he do?"

In answer, Grendel continued into the ragged settlement. Here and there he nodded at scared women and children. A few men of similar size to Grendel followed them, violence in their postures. However, they were more ragged than the tents they issued from, all slings and bandages, stumbling feet and labored breaths. Rust pitted the blades they carried, if they carried any at all. Even armorless and weaponless as he was, they were no threat to the greatest of the Geats.

The tents fell away and Grendel led him into a graveyard.

Dozens, perhaps hundreds, of runestones dotted the yard. Some old and pockmarked...most new, chisel marks still shiny in the ever-present light. A few mourners glanced up at their approach but disregarded them for their own grief.

"This is the business your debtor is in," Grendel said, voice hushed and reverent.

Beowulf swallowed, his thoughts returning to Hondscio's broken form on the ground of Heorot. No anger at the man next to him came with the memory, however. Only sadness at the loss. "Men die in war," he said. "I know this better than most."

Grendel scoffed. "This was not war. Hroðgar wanted our wealth. Gold and jewels, yes, but also our ancient connection to the One Eyed. He came to us with his spear-Danes under the guise of peace, and when we signed the treaty and a festival was thrown, his thanes rose up. They slew women and children where they slept, tortured the men to give up our secrets. Frig led us to this place, but Hroðgar is relentless. He sent his men fortnightly to raid and abduct, all for a secret Woden would never bestow."

"Hroðgar is a Godly man," Beowulf found himself saying. "He would not seek out the old ways."

Grendel eyed him, and Beowulf's stomach flipped. "Do you truly believe that?"

Beowulf could not answer.

Grendel peered over the field of his dead. "Woden answered my pleas and has given me the strength to fight back." He glanced at Beowulf. "Until now, at least."

"How do you do it?"

"Now you seek our secrets as well?"

Beowulf shook his head. "I have no need of otherworldly powers."

"No, I suppose you don't."

"How do you do it?"

Grendel sighed and ran a hand through his hair. Beowulf forced himself not to watch. "I sacrifice myself, and Woden gives. The power comes over me and I...change. Strength, fury, resilience." He smirked. "I was a farmer before all this. I never considered myself a violent man, but Tīw removes my better senses and frees me to do my gruesome purpose."

Beowulf's brow furrowed. War was the way of things. For glory and honor, wealth and land, war was the ultimate decider. But...

Hroðgar had kept this part of the story out, it seemed. The king had said the sceadugenga appeared after he built the great mead hall, a servant of the Enemy jealous of his success and prosperity, and for twelve long years the devil had stalked that hall.

He examined the man standing next to him. Grendel appeared around Beowulf's age, though weariness pulled down his posture. Could he really have kept up this solitary battle all that time?

Grendel caught him looking. "What goes through your mind, thane of Hygelac?"

Beowulf stepped away towards the nearest runestones. He needed space, his breath tight in his chest at the proximity of this man. "It's a heavy burden," he said, voice softer than he meant. "I go into battle with my dearest comrades, handpicked to weather any storm. You have waylaid Heorot for twelve years, with none at your side."

"Has it been that long?" Grendel said, almost to himself. "I am not entirely alone. My people still live, though we struggle. My mother is around." He gave a private smile. "She would burst through the doors of Heorot herself if I did not stop her."

"And yet you are lonely."

"Why do you say so?"

Beowulf shrugged. "As you pointed out, my trade is war. I know what it is like to stand in a shield wall with your brothers, and what it is like to face down a devil alone." He bowed his head. "I prefer the wall," he admitted to them both in a whisper. A secret he would never say aloud, even to his thirteen.

They watched each other for a long moment, neither speaking nor looking away. Beowulf's cheeks flushed as if from the strongest drink, and the urge to *move*, to *act*, was almost overwhelming.

"What will you do now, noble hero of Geatland?" Grendel said in a low voice. "Now that you know the whole of it."

Beowulf wet his lips, swallowed hard. "I don't know," he said truthfully. "I am sworn to repay the debt my father owed. Sworn to free Heorot from its tormentor."

A pause, then Grendel said, "But?"

"But I am also sworn before God Almighty to live with honor. There is honor in war, but not in...this." He motioned to the markers stretching before them.

Grendel stepped closer, and Beowulf's skin prickled at the proximity. The heat of the other man rolled off him like a smith's furnace. Whatever inner fire transformed him earlier—whether Woden's ancient blessing or a curse of the Enemy—was still burning strong.

"Then I ask again, great Beowulf," Grendel said, just loud enough to cross the span between them. "What will you do?"

Beowulf dared to turn. From here he could see a bit of gold in Grendel's dark brown eyes. The dry water had mussed his hair into curls that fell down his cheeks. Slight gray crept into his beard in stops and starts, prematurely for his apparent age. Beowulf wondered idly what Grendel saw when he looked at him. Did he see the hero Beowulf had become and was still becoming? Slayer of giants, sea creatures, and devils, afraid of nothing in this world, as powerful as thirty men?

Or did he see Beowulf as he truly was?

The soft expression in Grendel's eyes implied the latter.

Beowulf's chest tightened. "Will you leave this place? Flee to safety somewhere afield?"

Grendel shook his head. "It is not much, but this is our home. Hroðgar would not let us get far, regardless."

It was true. The king would never allow a defeat, even when victory would bring him nothing.

"I cannot raise my hand against Heorot," Beowulf said. "I will not break that oath."

Grendel nodded, a hint of sadness in his gaze. "I understand."

But he didn't. Not yet.

Iron resolve formed in Beowulf's chest, stronger than any bulwark. "I will not raise my hand against Heorot, but I will not stop *you* from doing so."

Grendel's eyes widened, then narrowed. "Why?" he said in a whisper.

"Because..." Beowulf searched for the right words. He shrugged. "I am Beowulf, son of Ecgtheow. Greatest of the Geats, or so some tell me. I will not be a pawn in King Hroðgar's crimes, not now I know the truth."

Grendel hesitated, inhaled, then took a final step forward. Beowulf's breath caught. "Then will you swear an oath to me?"

"Depends on the oath," Beowulf managed.

"Stay for a while," Grendel said. "Meet my people. See if they are worth your protection, as you believed Hroðgar to be."

So Beowulf did. Tentatively at first, as the people were clearly frightened of the mighty newcomer, but Grendel's presence at his side gave them confidence. He talked to the women and children of their fears and hopes, to the men of their rage and grief. He broke bread—what little there was—and shared his own stories. The young ones gasped and marveled at his deeds, while the elderly scoffed in disbelief.

The cavern was larger than he had originally suspected, though much of it was empty. Not enough people to fill the cold, dark corners.

And everywhere he went, Grendel was at his shoulder. Introducing his people by name, each looking to Grendel as a child to their parent.

"How long have you led them?" Beowulf asked at one point.

"Since after that first night," Grendel said. "Hroðgar burned down our hall, our leaders and fighting men inside."

This boiled Beowulf's blood. The utter dishonor of it, the cravenness. Nighttime raids were to be expected in war, but an ambush against a formal ally? And for what, some trinkets and the possibility of pagan powers?

By nightfall, Beowulf had seen enough, his heart simultaneously heavy and full. Grendel led him back to the pool he had come from, and they stopped, an easy silence falling.

"Thank you," Grendel said at length. "Thank you for listening."

Beowulf nodded, eyes on the still black water. "I am sorry for what happened to your people. I will pray to God for your sake."

Grendel smirked. "And I will pray to Woden for yours, Beowulf of the Geats."

They watched each other, something deep stirring in the pit of Beowulf's chest. Instincts that were never wrong propelled him forward. Grendel's eyes widened, hunger and longing plain.

Their kiss was fierce but short, Grendel's beard rough against his chin, his breath warm, a low sigh issuing from deep in his throat. Beowulf lived in that moment for a single heartbeat, allowed it to fill his soul.

Then he pulled away.

Grendel released a ragged exhale, lids fluttering open, lips slightly parted.

"I will ensure the king believes you are dead," Beowulf said. "You with all your people. He will return to his hall, confident in my victory. If you choose your time wisely, he will be drunk and vulnerable."

"This will stain your legacy," Grendel said. "The hero that *almost* killed the monster."

Beowulf grinned. "Maybe. Maybe not. Only time will tell, I suppose."

There was nothing more to say. Beowulf gave the sceadugenga a nod and dove into the water.

"Beowulf!" Aelfric said from the bottom of the hill. The sun was rising on the eastern horizon and still sounds of merriment were coming from the great hall in the distance. Aelfric ran to meet Beowulf, and they clapped shoulders. "How went the hunt?"

"Well, Aelfric," Beowulf said, clad once again in his mail cloak. "The creature is dead, as you suspected."

Relief washed over Aelfric's face but died when he saw Beowulf's expression. "What troubles you?"

"I am afraid," Beowulf said carefully, "we have been deceived." Aelfric became alert, his usual joviality replaced by cold attention. "Gather the men," Beowulf said in a hush. "We go to the king."

Aelfric nodded and ran off. Beowulf gazed up at the great hall, a monstrosity on the hill. He prodded the fire within his belly, stoking the rage just under the surface.

When he reached the newly boarded gates of the hall, his remaining thirteen stood behind him. They had donned mail and shield, sword and spear, helms upon their heads. Coiled violence was in their eyes.

The hall hushed when Beowulf's long shadow spilled from the doorway to the high table. Scylding thanes glanced around at each other in confusion and worry, reaching tentatively for weapons. The lady Wealhtheow saw them first, the surprise Beowulf expected quickly replaced with...anticipation?

Her king husband pawed lecherously at a serving maid next to his seat, oblivious to the Geats. Hroðgar's cheeks were ruddy with drink, his eyes unfocused. He only looked up when the maid stilled.

"Hail, King," Beowulf called. His voice boomed through the hall and the Scyldings recoiled.

"Son of Ecgtheow! You've returned." The king leaned forward and grinned. "Good tidings, I suspect?"

"The devil is dead," Beowulf said flatly. A murmur ran through the hall. Half-hearted cheers and claps of renewed joy were quickly replaced with concern.

Beowulf and his thirteen were neither cheering nor clapping.

Hroðgar finally seemed to sense the chill in the air. He licked his lips slowly. "Well met, hero of Hygelac," he said. "Do you bring proof of your deed?"

"My word is proof."

Hroðgar nodded. "That it is," he said with a slight slur. "That it is." He cleared his throat and leaned back, throwing his arms wide. "Then come! Come and join us. This is your celebration as much as mine."

"The devil is dead," Beowulf repeated, "as well as all of his people."

Confusion rippled into the crowd, glances and murmurs, though Beowulf's keen sight noticed some of the men did not share in the confusion. They gripped their weapons tighter.

"I see," Hroðgar said, eyes moving from Beowulf to his thirteen and back. "Very good."

"Tell me, King," Beowulf said. "Why would a God-fearing man such as yourself be seeking the blessings of the pagans?"

More confusion, and Hroðgar sputtered. "Are you already drunk, boy? Too much of my mead, loosening your tongue?"

Beowulf's temper flared then, and he stoked it higher. He took another step into the room and the great fire in the hearth seemed to dim in his presence. The thanes at the tables flinched away.

"The debt of my father is paid, but I regret now ever coming to this hall." He shook his head, rage burning in his throat. "I have seen the field of graves, *King*. Innocents, young and old alike. I have seen the proof of your deeds and your sins. I refuse to be party to your crimes any longer."

Hroðgar stood on wobbly legs, neck red with anger, and leaned two meaty hands on the table. "I will not be berated and accused by a —"

"I am Beowulf," he declared to the hall. "Son of Ecgtheow, thane of Hygelac, hero of the Geats, killer of the gaest Grendel." He scowled. "And I call you murderer. To deny it is to deny my honor." Fighting against the tension in his muscles, he placed his hand on the hilt at his waist. He lowered his voice so all in attendance had to lean in to hear. "Do you deny my honor?"

Hroðgar ground his teeth. His eyes bulged, moments from a drink-fueled eruption.

Beowulf met his gaze steadily.

No one moved. The fire crackled. A moment passed, then another.

"Get out of my hall," Hroðgar whispered. "Get out of my lands and never return."

Beowulf motioned to his men, and they began backing out the door. Beowulf glanced once more at the high table and its king. He gave a nod and followed into the early morning light.

"King Hygelac will not be pleased," Aelfric said next to him from the stern of their ship. They were a hundred yards from the coast, speeding north towards Geatland and home.

"He will understand," Beowulf said. "A few barrels of mead and Hroðgar will forget all about this little encounter."

Aelfric huffed. "You're probably right."

Barrels of mead, however, would likely be unnecessary.

Beowulf scanned the shrinking coastline before settling on a looming shape, dark against the lighter sands.

Two glowing pinpricks of smoldering red peered back across the waters.

Beowulf stood tall and met those eyes once more, held them for a long moment.

Finally, the figure turned away from the coast, back inland towards Heorot.

Lovers Leap

Lillian Barry

She holds me from behind. Strong hands grip my waist. My skin piques in the coastal air blowing from the window, but Geffray is a furnace. I bask in her heat, in our closeness. She warms me from behind.

When we first slept together, I thought I would hate myself for it. I thought she would fill me, mind and body, with all the women she'd bed before me.

But she only filled me with herself, and with the wooden toy I'd made for us. All my feelings tightened on me. My body rebirthed itself. She called me a woman, my own woman, and I came, shouting, into my own personhood.

Her hand slides down to my hip, and I must have made some noise of surprise or pleasure, because she laughs into my hair.

"What rouses you?" she asks as if it weren't her touching me in the first instance.

I cannot tell a truth she already knows. "It is near morning," I say instead.

"You'd be rid of me?" Her amusement rumbles in my ear.

I roll in her grip and kiss her hard on the mouth. "I will not have my uncle catch you making a dishonest woman out of me."

I love Geffray's smile. Her crooked teeth almost look straight in the tilt of her parted lips.

It's gone now.

"I'd rather be free," she says. Her gaze slips past me, sucked out the open window along with the tatty drapes and all the warmth in the room.

"Then be free and cold," I say testily, pulling away from her embrace. "And I'll stay warm here under the blanket."

She gets out of bed and I'm immediately reminded that it's cold here without her. She takes her heat with her. I wish she'd leave some for me. I wish I could accept it if she did.

"I thought it was you kicking me out, not me choosing to leave you." She stands over me and an echo of her earlier amusement returns. "Come with me, Auriol."

The endless sky is overcast in a way that promises open space and uncertainty, likely rain. Besides, I am wearing nothing but a thin nightdress and I fear the wind will rip me to shreds.

"I will not," I say. But I'm desperate now to take back my doubts and fears. Geffray does not deserve them. "Come back to bed?" I plead.

Geffray does not regard me long. But neither does she buckle her studded belt and vault the window, as she usually does. Perhaps she sniffs the contrition between my legs. She is too gallant to leave me in my misery.

She grabs my bare ankles and yanks me down the bed.

"You will learn to attend to yourself," she growls, right before she ducks under the blanket.

My uncle finds us here a few minutes later. Me stifling a wail in my fists, breasts out, legs apart. Geffray nought but a headless kneeling figure.

"Whore!" my uncle screams at me.

If I had any thoughts in that moment, I would have kept Geffray concealed and bid my uncle leave while I said farewell to my supposedly male lover. Perhaps my uncle would have allowed that.

Instead, I pull the blanket to cover my breasts, only to bare Geffray's glistening face and invoke my uncle's horror.

"Witch!" he hisses. "You should not be here."

I am prone and frozen. How many months have I avoided discovery, only to be caught now? In my first heartbeat I blame Geffray for seducing me. In my second I curse my uncle for tormenting her.

But Geffray rocks back on her heels and wipes her mouth with her sleeve. If it were just me watching, she would use a rag or her hand. But she always acts uncouth under the watch of those who hate her. Acting proper would not change their minds, she tells me. Just this once, I wish she would not provoke my uncle so.

"You should not be in your niece's bedroom," she says.

And I marvel at her afresh. Though there is no real privacy in my uncle's house, with him and my eight cousins, I have heard things from other girls in the village that make me feel lucky.

My uncle, while he won't hurt me—though he called me a whore—looks fit to hit Geffray.

"It is my house," he says. "But I meant that you should not be on this island. You are a witch, you were born to a witch, you belong with the witches."

"On the rock in the bay whence you banished them?" Geffray scoffs.

"Your mothers went willingly."

I look between them. While I am half exposed, their conversation cloaks them in some knowledge I do not share. My uncle knew Geffray's mother? Her mothers? All I know is Geffray is the offspring of a witch. Born on the satellite island a few miles off the cliffside, she swam here as a young woman seeking work and friendship. She found one of the two, with the men in the quarry; friends she lacked for a long time, until she began to meet women and women began to meet her.

I am not sure if we are friends, exactly, in the traditional sense, but I suspect I am not the only one who loves her.

"You can exile me if you like, but I will not go," Geffray says.

My uncle squares her off. Though she is still on the floor, and he looms above, she does not budge.

"Very well." My uncle leans down and swipes her discarded belt from the floor. "There are other means."

And he leaves, belt in hand.

Geffray sighs and tilts her head from side to side. Click. Click. *Crack.* Then she turns up the blanket once again.

"Where were we?"

"Geffray!" I admonish. "You have to go! I'm sure he's going to the constable!"

"I don't care."

She gives me her devilish smile—the one I can't get enough of—and despite myself I'm laughing.

"Lie back down, Auriol. I'll show you how witches' daughters do it."

———◦◦———

I was right. My uncle went straight to the constable with Geffray's studded belt. I think she was expecting it, because instead of going to the quarry for her workday as usual, she lingered in the village. She is still washing her hands and face at the well when I pass on my way to Janie's.

"There's the strange person again," my little cousin Ari, who isn't old enough to go to school with the others, says. "Why is she looking at you like that, Aura?"

I glance up. Meeting Geffray's crooked grin is akin to falling. But instead of a pleasant surrender, as it was earlier, I feel horror. Like the earth is crumbling beneath my feet. Every time I look at her in public, I risk the world finding out what we are to each other and casting us away because of it.

But it is her looking at me now, risking the same. Carefully, carelessly, she rakes her eyes up my calves and under my skirt. She is so obvious. It feels like a taunt, perhaps for me and perhaps for the world.

I wish she would not.

"Come inside now, Ari."

I usher my cousin into Janie's house, where the village women have gathered to make jam today. Ari scampers off with the other children, not heeding my caution not to soil her clothes with berry juice. I am left with the women.

"Auriol, we heard what happened," Janie begins. She pulls out a stool and pushes me to sit. "In your own home! I can't believe it!"

I recoil from the perceived rebuke. Really, I should not have come here.

"Who was the rascal?" Valery chimes in. "I will beat his head in with a pestle."

My tense muscles begin to unwind. Perhaps my uncle kept the details to himself. An altered story will be easier to shrug off.

But Janie returns, "Oh, Val, you missed the latest. It was not a man. It was Geffray. They have her belt as evidence."

Silence falls like a shroud over my honour.

I flush with shame.

"Geffray! But she's outside," Valery hisses. "At the well. Right this moment!"

I have known these women all my life. I have spent more hours in their company than time spent alone. Of late, I have begun to feel apart from them. More and more, I drift away during their chatter. The talk always comes back around to the men in their lives. And that irks me, for it interrupts my thoughts of Geffray.

But what Elsi whispers now brings me right back into their midst.

"She promised she would never get caught." Elsi presses a hand to her heart.

I hate her for it.

The other women tut and shush. They're waiting for me to speak, but they won't look at me.

"What did she promise, Elsi?" My throat is folding in on itself, trying to create a sob or a bite.

Elsi hiccups. She is closer to crying than I. *Good.*

"She promised that whenever I need her, she will be there. But if she's been caught, that's it. She'll never visit me again. It's *over.*"

I glance at the others, but Janie, with her hand still on my shoulder from when she made me sit, is the only one who'll touch me.

"Here, Auriol, don't say you didn't know."

"Who else?" It comes out as a grunt.

"Oh…" Even Janie lets go, as if my creeping rage burned her.

"Who *else*?" Now it's a bark.

And Valery puts her hand up.

Shock takes the place of fury, then embarrassment of them both. The fight drains out of me.

"She doesn't visit my bed any more," says Valery. "But I…"

I wait.

Janie prods her in the arm. "Say it, Val."

"I think I will always be a little bit in love with her."

I press hot fingers to my aching temples and long for the wind to suck me outside like it did the curtains this morning.

"I knew she slept with others," I say, because I can't stand them all looking at me like this, like they pity me, like they pity themselves for betraying me. "When she's with me, though, I don't think of anyone else. It's easy to pretend it's just us. Just…me."

I am alone after all.

As I'm speaking, a shout echoes between the stone cottages. We crowd to the window, and through the hole we see the constable marching up to the well with two of the village men. Rotten men, the lot of them.

Geffray's gaze ticks towards Janie's house over their shoulders. Her grin surfaces when she sees me peeking through the window. Or maybe *us*. Elsi and Val and maybe even Janie too. She knows we're watching.

"Geffray, you are under arrest!" booms the constable.

"For what?" asks Geffray mildly.

"A crime against a woman!" The constable is known to be a proud defender of women.

Val, beside me, makes a gagging noise in her throat.

"I see." Geffray's laugh is louder than any judgment. "Well, good luck with that."

The constable turns as purple as the jam we're supposed to be making. "You're sentenced to death!" he declares.

Geffray laughs again. "I don't think so."

"Men have been executed for lesser deeds."

"Do you think?"

Janie is shaking her head crossly. Yes, indeed, the constable is a proud defender of women.

"What, exactly, is my crime?" says Geffray. It's not a question as much as a dare. "You cannot arrest me without saying it out loud."

"You fucked a woman!" The constable's voice peaks like a boy's. "We have evidence."

"Keep your evidence."

Geffray slowly turns her head once again to regard us in the window. But this time I get the feeling she's speaking directly to me.

"I fucked her indeed. I fucked her with my fingers and I fucked her with my mouth, and I fucked her with the wooden toy she made for me."

I feel her everywhere. Her hot breath, her firm stroke; my arching back, my beating core.

The next time I'm fit to look out the window, her hands are cuffed behind her back and the men are leading her to the holding cell on the cliff.

"Sentenced to death?" Elsi has gone pale as a split stone. "Surely not."

"It's all bluster, no brains," Janie assures her. "There is no such crime as a woman lying with a woman."

"Then why does my uncle glare upon it so?" I find myself musing. "If it is not a crime?"

"It's supposed to be unnatural. Like it doesn't exist," says Valery.

"But I've done it," I insist. "*You've* done it."

The others shrug.

"I'd deny it," said Elsi. "I *do* deny it. I don't want to die."

Janie throws her hands in exasperation, but not one of us says we'd do differently.

———⟡———

It's mid afternoon by the time I can take Ari home and leave her with her older siblings. I tell them I won't be gone long—but as

I walk away from the village and up the hill, dread burns in my thighs. I fear there is no returning. Or if there is, that I will be alone.

There are no guards near the holding cell. The cell is gouged into the hillside, metal bars looking out to the ocean. As I round the bank it occupies, I spy a single figure locked up inside. She slumps against the wall, eyes hooded.

"Geffray!" I cry out. "Let's get you out of there!"

She straightens as she spots me, and a slow grin curls across her bruised face.

"My love, there is no getting out," she says lazily. "The constable has the keys."

"Then I will dig you out," I declare.

"It is solid rock all round. Don't think I haven't looked."

"But you haven't," I point out. Her hands and feet are chained and she looks barely conscious. As much as it crushes my heart to see her hurt, I am bleeding with shame that I must see her weak.

She laughs, though.

"I will not run," she says. "I have done nothing I wouldn't do again."

"The constable wants you to be..." I cannot say it.

"Executed." The word feels soft in her mouth, somehow—or sad, like something wanted and inevitable.

My feet stutter and I sink to the ground. Tears fall from my eyes in a great, silent river.

Geffray shuffles closer to the bars, and I reach through to clutch her bound hands. Her skin is clammy like dew, but her blood hums. The furnace within is still burning.

"I have done nothing I wouldn't do again," she repeats. "They cannot charge me as a man because I am not one. They can't charge me as a woman because there is no such crime."

"That's what Janie said."

I watch her face carefully: the little uptick of her mouth, the subtle crinkle of her eyes.

"Janie too?" I ask her.

She rouses at that, and regards me with curiosity. "You didn't know?"

"Of course I didn't know."

She shakes her head now, and sweat drips from her hair. "Women should talk to each other."

"Should they fuck each other too?" I retort.

"Auriol…"

"What?" I let go of her hands.

She tilts at the touch withdrawn, and I notice the smear of blood on the wall behind her. She has been whipped. Her own belt, the evidence used against her, lies across the cell. The studs are dull and brown with blood.

I squeeze my eyes shut.

Click. Click. *Crack*.

Geffray speaks again, low, a beautiful rumble like water in a cave.

"Listen, Auriol. You are beautiful. You are kind. You are full of feeling. These are strengths within you. Now take your strengths and let them make you strong. Declare who you are. Take your leap of passion. I may be gone by the time you start your own journey, but remember I have every faith in your spirit."

"Gone?" Panic tightens around my throat. "You said you cannot be charged."

"I would love to take the leap with you, if you would take it with me," she says, not answering me.

But I find I cannot speak. I am not ready for a journey. My passions are private. My feelings are inconsequential. Like Elsi, I will deny and keep denying if it will save the life I have.

Geffray drops her gaze. I feel like we are separated by an ocean.

"She cannot be charged as a woman or a man…" A deep, cruel voice cuts any intimacy we once shared into ribbons. "…But she can be charged as a witch."

I stare as the constable clomps up the mound to stand on top of the cell. He smirks down at me and Geffray, huddled up to the bars.

"She will be tried by the hangman at daybreak!" he hollers loud enough for the entire village to hear. "Now leave her, whore!"

He cocks his baton at my head, and I scramble to my feet.

I scarcely throw a backward glance at Geffray's crumpled form as I run away. I scarcely hear her bellow after me: "Yes, Aura, women *should* fuck each other!"

⁕

I dream of Geffray's embrace, but when I wake, there is nobody there.

Cold and heavy, my bones made of stone, I follow my uncle and cousins up the hill. Everyone is here: my friends and their families, the constable holding Geffray's chains, and even the hangman leaning on the hilt of his axe.

She kneels, barely wobbling, chin high. She does not smile when she sees me, but the sunrise glints devilishly in her eyes. I am not sure whether I am afraid for her or of her.

"What's the accusation?" the hangman booms.

"She assaulted a woman," says the constable.

"Who brings the charge?"

"I am the victim's guardian." My uncle steps forward, leaving my cousins to throng me like meadowflowers around a treestump. "I saw it with my own eyes."

The hangman yawns. "That is not a crime."

The constable speaks up. "Only a witch would assault a woman."

Shock ripples through the crowd.

"A witch, you say?" The hangman swings his axe like a toy on a string.

"She was born to witches," my uncle adds. "We all know this. And to assault my niece, I believe she must be one herself."

The hangman's gaze snaps to me.

"Did this woman assault you?" he asks me.

My head pounds. Geffray regards me from her prone position a tomato's throw away.

"No," I say.

The crowd stirs. The hangman shrugs. A vein pulses in my uncle's forehead.

"As the victim's guardian, I insist," says my uncle. "The witch has to die."

"She will die for being a witch, not for sleeping with a woman," says the hangman. "But let it be clear that women who willingly sleep together might as well be witches."

He looks directly at me again, and I stumble backward. Ari hides in my skirt. I feel I should be the one hiding.

The hangman does not ask me again. But he does call out: "For being a witch, Geffray will be thrown off this cliff into the sea."

My heart stops beating. Images dizzy through my mind: Geffray on the floor, Geffray between my legs, Geffray behind bars, Geffray hurtling through thin air to jagged rocks and sharp surf.

My pulse returns hard and fast. My body clenches around the shock and numbs it enough that I can stumble with the other villagers to the cliff-edge, where the constable has dragged my lover and uncuffed her under the hangman's orders. I bite my tongue and taste iron. Can I offer my blood for her life? I babble a prayer in my mind.

"Last words?" asks the hangman.

Geffray finds my eyes once again. She presses her hot lips together.

"So be it."

The hangman pushes her, and she disappears.

Someone screams. Maybe it's me. I drop to the ground and crawl to the edge, desperate for a glimpse of her body. But she's not in the air and I can't find her in the roiling sea below. She's already gone.

It feels like the water is closing in on my own head. It fills my ears and lungs. I can't breathe. I gasp, but I don't know if I want to breathe, or if I want to follow her.

Rough hands drag me back from the edge. Voices bubble around me. It takes a long time, but eventually my heart slows and my hearing clears. The crowd has not dispersed; there is an air of waiting, and I am not sure if it is for me, or the other bodies of fainting women who have fallen with shock, or the sense of unease that has sprung up around this hasty trial and execution.

But all this melts away at the shout my cousin Ari lets out.

"The strange person is swimming!" she cries.

And everyone bolts to the cliff-edge once again.

My vision is blurry, but even I spy the lone swimmer confidently crawling back to shore.

"She fell without injury," mutters Janie.

"She swims like a witch, too," my uncle growls.

Steady footsteps thump up the cliff path from the bay. Geffray looks weak no longer. Wet, she is handsome, swashbuckling. Layers of clothing contour her broad shoulders and thick stomach. Her studded belt, now restored to her, frames her hips. Seawater drips down her windburnt face and salt crusts her hair. And she's smiling her crooked smile and *fuck*—

"She lives!" cries the crowd.

"How can it be?"

"Fate smiles upon her."

"What a marvellous feat!"

Other women—not just me and Elsi—are swooning and fanning themselves.

"We must pardon and free her," says one of the matriarchs.

My uncle looks fit to combust.

"Enough!" he calls. "The witch was sentenced to death. I will accept no pardon!"

The hangman shakes his head. "She was sentenced to be thrown off the cliff and she survived her sentence. The case is closed."

But Geffray strides to my uncle and presents her empty palms. "How about this?" she says. "I'll jump. If I survive, I go free."

My uncle stares. He knows she is mocking him.

The hangman guffaws. "I have never seen anyone survive once, let alone twice," he says. "But I like a game. On behalf of the victim's guardian, I accept."

My uncle fumes—he does not like games, or when people do things on his behalf—but he is getting his way, after all. Geffray is sure to die this time around.

She walks to the cliff-edge herself this time. There are no bindings to be undone. The knot around my throat loosens. This time, she will not be pushed. She will jump.

And she does.

Geffray takes a running leap off the cliff. Her lithe body arcs in a dive. She seems to hover there, and I fancy she winks at me between her outstretched arms.

Then she's going down, down, cutting through the air like a bird, or maybe a dolphin. We all watch her fall.

A sick feeling churns in my stomach as she reaches the water. But she seems to cleave it in two and vanish without a splash. It's only a few agonising seconds before she resurfaces, flicks the hair out of her eyes, and begins the strong crawl back to shore once again.

The crowd cheers and I'm cheering with them. She's alive! Again! Valery and Elsi cling to my sides and we celebrate together.

Geffray hauls herself back up the cliff path amidst claps and whoops. I note the way she rolls her neck—a tiny sign of fatigue that no one else would catch. But her smile stretches far and wide.

"Are you satisfied?" she asks my uncle.

Far from defeated, my uncle is smirking. "It is unnatural," he says loudly enough for all to hear, "unnatural to dodge certain death! Her survival sneers at our humanity!"

"Hear, hear!" the constable agrees.

The celebrations are over. To the crowd, my uncle makes a compelling argument.

We quieten and turn anxious gazes to the hangman.

He is swinging his axe once again. Hot and bitter, bile pools in the pit of my belly.

"I agree it is unnatural. But justice is the will of the people. Let us hear from them." The hangman addresses the crowd. "The woman is clearly a witch. Do you want her to live?"

Some heads shake. Most of the women stand frozen. They loved her first survival, when she defied death and made a mockery of judgment, all within the rules of the lawmakers. The second time is a different matter. The gall of her, to jump of her own accord! The unconscionable disregard for her own life! And for it to pay off—well, to the villagers as to my uncle, it is proof of witchery. No divine entity would let Geffray get away with that gamble.

But for me, it is as if Geffray's bold leap lit a fire deep within me. The men's posturing and game-playing stoke it; their fickle words are my fuel. The women's attraction and respect for Geffray resolve me; their ultimate cowardice is our tragedy. Heat spreads from my core to my skin, from my tips to my toes.

Geffray speaks up. "My dear enemies, I no longer care if you want me to live. My friends and lovers know I deserve to. I will jump again, and this time I will not return."

Rage curls my fists, vibrates on my tongue. And now I am opening my mouth too.

"Then I will jump with her!" I cry. "If you would have her gone, I will go too!"

The crowd gasps. Elsi whimpers at my side, but does not speak.

"You fool!" Valery hisses.

"Hangman, please, pardon them both," Janie appeals.

The hangman fixes me with a glare sterner than any I have ever faced. "I'll ask again. Did the woman assault you?"

I flex my fingers and answer: "No!"

The hangman proclaims, "They are both witches. Let them both die if they would die together."

The people roar—with approval or in protest, I cannot tell—as I march to Geffray's side.

My uncle watches with teeth locked in a snarl. My cousins are wide-eyed. My friends are weeping.

And Geffray...Geffray clasps my hand in her own.

Click. Click. *Crack.*

"Do not fear," she murmurs in my ear. "We will swim to the island where I grew up. My mothers will take care of us."

"The island of witches?" I ask.

I feel rather than see her nod.

"Then we will both be witches," I say.

"Here, we are witches. There, we are whatever we want to call ourselves."

"Last words?" asks the hangman. He steps closer, his axe barring the way back to safety.

We press our lips together.

Hand in hand, we turn. The ocean stretches far below and far into the distance.

She counts down. We step forward, bracing our knees, then jump.

Nothingness envelops me. I am neither here nor there, on land nor sea, accepted nor rejected, witch nor mortal, alive nor dead.

There is not time to fear the swim ahead before strong, familiar hands grip my waist. My skin piques in the cool air blowing from the horizon, but Geffray is a furnace, and I am one too. I bask in our heat, in our closeness. She warms me from behind and I warm her from in front.

She whips me into her arms. She cradles me, her body my hammock, and together we pitch into the sea.

So Many Times Undone

Hailie Kei

Act I: Terror

1793

On a dark night, down a dark narrow lane, within an even darker city, a corner house hosted a private meeting at the peak of dark times. In this house sat a young woman of barely nineteen, and within her was a darkness deeper than them all.

If asked to describe Liliane-Marie Dubois, her Uncle Henri would say she was a kind and intelligent girl despite having the misfortune of being born mute. If one were to ask the priest Father Faucher, he would describe Liliane as the cambion demon spawn of an incubus and Henri's late deranged sister. He would also say that her mutism was a curse so that she could never cry out for God's mercy on the day of judgment.

Neither man was wrong.

On this night, the one that would change the course of her death—and life thereafter—Liliane was dutifully recording the minutes of another meeting of Girondin supporters at her uncle's home as they plotted over a table littered with political pamphlets and newspapers. As always, her uncle and Father Faucher were arguing. The recent assassination carried out by a fellow member, and her subsequent beheading, had not hindered Henri's pursuit of their cause, but bolstered it. He continued to host small meetings which became more desperate by the week. However, as Liliane transcribed their feverish proclamations, she could not ease the fear that they were all on the wrong side of the revolution erupting in Paris.

After the meeting, Liliane helped the housemaid, Colette, tidy up after the men who'd returned to their homes or lay asleep drunk in the drawing room like her uncle. The heavy sense of foreboding slowed Liliane's movements as she swept the floor of pipe ash and torn papers. Colette came behind her, taking her hand gently.

"You seem tired," said Colette, "I'll prepare your bed."

A flush of heat prickled Liliane's skin as she gave a nod of thanks, smiling as she turned away with the broom, giving a final two sweeps, before quietly following the housemaid up the stairs.

Once Liliane closed the door to her room, Colette undressed her, starting with the pins in her hair, letting her dark curls fall past the nape of her pale neck. Liliane shuddered as Colette placed her lips against her neck as her fingers deftly undid the stays of her black bodice. As the garment fell, Colette's soft hands cupped Liliane's breasts with familiar tenderness. Liliane turned to meet the face of her lover and brushed her thumb across her flushed round cheek before leaning in to kiss her open mouth.

"One day you will tell me you love me."

Colette's words came almost an hour later as she and Liliane lay together in the bed. Sweat from silent exertion and the summer heat sticking to their skin.

"If there is only one thing you ever speak in your life," Colette continued, "I selfishly wish it is that."

Liliane put her arm around Colette's soft stomach and held her close, but her lover was stiff in her embrace. Liliane licked her lips which were still swollen and tangy from kisses and pleasure. The words formed a knot in her chest but would not go further. Likewise, her mouth opened, only to close, defeated by her curse.

Colette was about to speak, but a rapid knocking from below followed by a clamor of angry voices stopped her. Both women scrambled out the bed, Liliane taking the sheet with her as Colette gathered her clothing. From below her window, Liliane could see a group of men pushing their way through the front door. Her blood ran cold. It wasn't the first time, but Liliane knew it would be the last. Liliane pushed Colette half-dressed towards the balcony window, the only escape.

"Come with me!" Colette cried, as she stepped onto the balcony. "This is not your fight!"

Liliane hesitated. If not her uncle's cause, what was her fight? Her world was so small that she could not think beyond midnight meetings and talks of revolution and conspiracy. She could not fathom a life beyond this little house and her quiet duties.

"Liliane, please!"

The bedroom door flew open, and Liliane startled backwards as three men in red wool caps carrying muskets came in. Shock replaced the determined looks on their faces as their eyes shifted from the garments on the floor to Liliane naked but for her bedsheet, then to the blanched-faced girl scaling out the window.

Liliane shut the window as Colette descended the trellis. One man shouted at the others to stop Colette, and as they scrambled off, he demanded that Liliane cover herself before he entered. But she stood there, frozen, sheet clenched in her hand. The man averted his eyes for a moment, then looked at her directly.

"Liliane-Marie Dubois. You are under arrest."

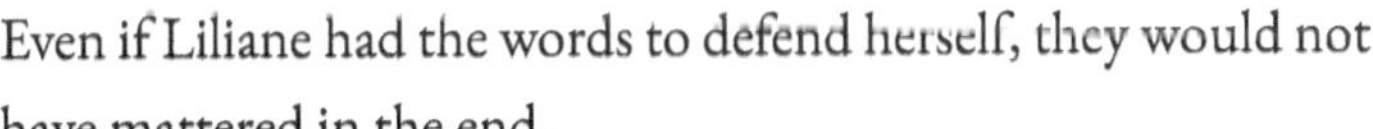

Even if Liliane had the words to defend herself, they would not have mattered in the end.

Her uncle and other members had proclaimed her innocence during their trials. For the first time Henri had referred to his ward as a simpleton, an illegitimate dunce unable to speak or write, who had spent her quiet life in ignorance of the group's activities. But Liliane was twice damned when the prosecutor matched her handwriting in records of the meetings to explicit personal diary entries and salacious letters to the housemaid who was yet to be found. There were talks in defense of having her committed to an institution, but in the end, allegations of treason and conspiracy outweighed those of tribadism and nymphomania, and Liliane was sentenced to death.

<hr>

On the night before her execution, Liliane regretted her hesitation to run away and truly live for herself. She wrote a final diary entry in the paper the prison guards had allowed her. She considered all that was taken from her, from the warm bed with her lover, and all hope for a future, and wrote them down.

Pleasure, love, and the power to choose my own destiny.

An owl cooed in the high window of Liliane's cell, the only companion who had not been taken to the guillotine during the four months of her imprisonment. She bade it goodnight with a bow for the last time, clasped the paper in her palms, and closed her weary eyes.

Liliane startled awake to the sensation of a dull weight pushing against her supine body. She couldn't move anything but her eyes. She watched with horror as the twilight shadows of her room pooled together, forming a large black wolfish dog astride her chest, red eyes boring into hers. Beside it sat a man in a black coat, sallow skinned and bearded, with a narrow, hooked nose, and familiar, round owlish eyes the color of brimstone framed by hair which moved like feathers. A sly smile curved his lips.

"Good evening, daughter."

Liliane tried to scream, to move, to get away from the man, but her efforts were in vain. All she could do was blink back the tears that formed in her eyes. Father Faucher had been right, and now she would suffer the same fate as her mother at the hands of this incubus.

"I am Andras, Marquis of hell," said the demon, his voice low and even. "I've not come to harm you, but to save you. I am but a doting father willing to fulfill his ill-fated daughter's last desires."

The demon leaned in and stroked Liliane's sweat-damp hair with long cold fingers.

"You wish for a life beyond the blade of the guillotine," he whispered. "Bind yourself to me and I will give you all you ask for"—he tapped the paper still clenched in her paralyzed hand—"*and more. All I ask is we make a small bargain. Blink twice if you accept.*"

Liliane tried to steady her beating heart, but it pounded with the desire to live and have all the demon offered her, no matter the cost.

She blinked once, a tear streaming down her cheek, then twice.

The demon pulled a single ribbon of red velvet from his coat and tied it around Liliane's neck.

"We are bound," Andras stated as he stood. "I'll see you after your execution."

Shadows swept in from the corners of the cell, surrounding the demon in a cloak of black feathers until he and the hellhound were gone.

Liliane bolted upright in her bed, thrashing and rubbing the chill from her skin with frantic hands. Rays of sunlight crept into her cell, dispelling the shadows, and the terrible nightmare.

A dream, it had been a dream.

Liliane's relief was tinged by a prickle of disappointment, at the dangerous hope beyond the fate she would meet in a few hours. She ran both hands through her shorn hair then down to her neck and paused, a fresh panic rising in her chest as her fingers brushed against something soft and smooth.

She tugged at the velvet ribbon around her neck but could not unbind it.

⸺⊛⸻

It was only fitting that the spawn of a demon would be executed on Halloween.

Liliane imagined Father Faucher would say as much if his head weren't at the bottom of a basket with her uncle's. Her own head, and this strange, cursed ribbon the guards could not undo would soon join them. Liliane approached the scaffold, arms bound, tears blurring the hundreds of faces filling the Place de la Révolution public square on this dreary afternoon. She raised her face to the elevated blade as she approached it, its sharp angled edge stained red with the priest's blood. The executioner lowered Liliane's neck face-down into the slick wooden cradle of the stocks. She raised her eyes to the clamoring crowd whose voices and shouts became a buzz as she focused on the black dog standing silently between them, staring back at her with eyes that flickered with the fires of hell as the rope above her unspooled.

Liliane's world shifted, a sudden sidewards tilt on its axis.

A soft thud, the stench of musk, blood, a deep cold, then a final, silent descent of darkness.

Act II: Pleasure
1793—1803

Upon waking for the first time since her death on a bed in an unfamiliar room, Liliane-Marie Dubois was horrified to find that beneath her tidy red ribbon was an equally unfamiliar body.

She screamed, and with it came a voice for the first time. The demon Andras was there to catch her before she swooned, and reassure her that all was well. He explained that he had taken her severed head with him to Austria beyond the grasp of the revolutionaries, and had found her the body of a lovely Austrian woman with a voice unsullied by a curse—yes, the priest had been right about that too—and, as promised, he would give Liliane everything she asked for: pleasure, love, and power.

"This body you inhabit will only last one year. Over time, it will lose sensation, die and begin to rot," said the demon as he stroked the massive head of his hellhound. "To keep on living, you must replace your body each year on your death day. To do so, you will need a body—a living one—and get them alone during the witching hours of October 31st. Then you will undo the ribbon around your neck, and I will come to claim their soul for my hell court. In return, I will give you their body. A few stipulations. The ribbon can only be undone on Halloween, and only by you. The only way someone else can undo it is if you ask them to and in this case, it will be *your* soul I drag to hell, effectively ending our contract. Any questions?"

"How..." Liliane uttered, testing her new voice. She touched her throat with an unfamiliar hand, meeting the ribbon there and flinching. "How long must I do this?"

Andras shrugged. "As long as you like. A year, a millennium. It makes no difference to me. You may have as many lives as you wish." He stood, and the hellhound stood with him. "For now, I give you *Pleasure*." He gestured to the ornate room with its silk canopied bed, velvet walls, and gold framed mirrors. "Enjoy."

As soon as the doors opened, sounds of passionate moans and drunken laughter flooded in from the hall. An older woman with a powdered wig and face replaced Andras in the doorway and beamed at Liliane wide-eyed on the satin bed-sheets.

"Oh! She's lovely!" she cried in French, pressing her hand to her full bosom. "You'll do well here, very well indeed."

⸻◈⸻

Madame LeCourt's pleasure house, Le Petit Bijou in Vienna, catered to aristocratic French émigrés who intended to keep up the lifestyle they were persecuted for and use their political asylum as an indefinite holiday. In addition to sex, Madame LeCourt offered her high-end clients luxurious boarding, parties, and gambling. But they bored easily, and the matron was running out of ways to keep them entertained and decided a fresh face was in order. Andras was there to give her one in the form of Liliane, with a promise of business success for as long as the girl was employed. As always, there was a contingency, and in this case, it was to allow Liliane to request anything she desired and refuse anything she did not. Despite this, Liliane proved to be a popular addition to Madame LeCourt's courtesans. To the aristocrats, Liliane's ubiquitous blood-red velvet ribbon appeared to be a cheeky ode to the guillotine and soon became a vulgar fashion trend amongst them.

When Liliane had wished for pleasure, it had been a vague fantasy, an extension of her brief time with Colette, but now, in this secret club where dreams were met for a cost, the possibilities were endless. Liliane stating her preference for the female sex opened a niche market for Madame LeCourt. Her first client was a shy noblewoman named Eloise. Liliane had been insecure in her previous body, it had been thin and flat, but her current body had full breasts and sensual hips, and she was determined to enjoy it. By the end of the night, neither woman was unsatisfied, but once alone, Liliane cried for her Colette. The noblewoman, Eloise, became a regular, and Liliane soon had a steady clientele. Not all women were shy, some were bold, some liked to be dominated, and some did not appear to be women until they undressed. Liliane enjoyed them all and rarely turned anyone or their inclinations away. She even took a man to bed once but was underwhelmed, and politely declined the next gentleman who asked.

Pleasure, it turned out, went beyond sexual gratification. Liliane developed a sweet tooth for cakes and candies of all kinds. With her new voice, she spoke often, impressing others with the cleverness and intelligence she'd never been able to articulate. She went to the theater, orchestra, and social salons among Vienna's elite. Soon she too was wrapped up in a luxurious life of blissful ignorance while Paris continued to bleed.

Pleasure was the freedom of gluttonous sensation and Liliane spent months eating her fill.

But her ignorance did not last long, for, almost eight months into her new life, she slowly began to die. The change was subtle, a tingle in her fingers that would dull to numbness. A client's kiss that went unnoticed. A warm bath that felt like an empty cavern. Then, at last on the week before her death day, the sickening sensation of being completely untethered from the world around her, of being nothing but a bit of neck and a head.

Liliane kept to her room for the week and received no visitors. It wasn't until the night of October 31st that she finally asked for company. Eloise entered Liliane's room with a concerned arch of her fine eyebrows.

"How are you, Lily? Madame LeCourt says you are unwell."

Liliane reached towards Eloise from the bed where she lay propped up on pillows. Every movement she made seemed like a form of sorcery; an action performed by a mental puppet string. Eloise took her hand and joined her on the bed. Liliane expected to feel something but realized that all the sensations of doubt and fear were absent. She could not even feel the rapid beat of her heart to express her anxiety. She cleared her throat, and her voice came out hoarse and in a whispery rasp.

"I'm sorry..." she uttered, bringing her hand to the ribbon at her throat, using the pressure against her upper neck to guide her fingers as she closed her eyes. "I've always admired your figure." She pulled at the velvet bow and slowly drew it down until it was undone.

Eloise screamed as Liliane's head tumbled to the floor.

Liliane blinked rapidly in a panic but felt no pain other than the dull impact with the carpet. She could not turn from the image of Andras manifesting in the room cloaked in swirling shadows, snarling hellhound at his feet, longsword in hand. Eloise stumbled off the bed and tried to run, but the dog grabbed her ankle with its sharp fangs, dragging her to the floor. As she lifted her head to cry out, Andras came behind her, and with one clean sweep cut Eloise's head from her shoulders. The hellhound loped after it like a puppy, tail wagging as it brought the head to its master, but was scolded and told to drop it with a firm command.

Andras gently picked up Liliane's head, viscous blood spilling through his fingers, and brought it to the body across the room. He placed the top half of Liliane's neck on the bottom of Eloise's like a doll maker and deftly tied the ribbon around them.

Liliane shot upright, a rush of heat filling her from head to toe as she felt the moment her new heart began to beat for the first time. Liliane had a new body, a new voice afflicted with Eloise's accent, but most of all, a new chance at life. And, as she sat in a pool of blood and stared back at Eloise's empty eyes, she felt nothing but the hunger to keep on living.

The second time was not as terrible, and nor was the third.

By the fourth one, damning innocent souls to hell to keep living became routine. Liliane continued her life of luxury and pleasure at Le Petit Bijou for a decade without aging a day since her death. Following the end of the beheadings and the Reign of Terror, many patrons of Le Petit Bijou returned to France, but Liliane did not follow. Despite her years with the Girondins, now politics stirred nothing in her. Away from home, she felt disconnected in both body and spirit from the girl who had silently called for justice, women's rights, and abolition. Liliane had become what she had despised, and it wasn't long before she lost all sense of pleasure far before her body did.

It was time to leave Le Petit Bijou and her vapid Austrian social life.

Madame LeCourt had begged her to stay. She knew that her business depended on Liliane's employment. But Liliane could not be dissuaded, and once she left, a rapid outbreak of syphilis closed Le Petit Bijou for good.

Despite experiencing pleasure in all its forms, there was an emptiness that lingered after each sexual encounter. An emptiness that had never been there when Liliane lay in Colette's arms. A spark of hope in her most recent chest filled her with longing. And, ten years after her death, Liliane-Marie Dubois returned to France in search of Love.

Act III: Love

1803—1804

It took months to find Colette.

Before leaving Vienna, Liliane had specifically chosen a body closest to her own ten years ago. She'd hoped to return to her lover with full feeling and a warm body, but it was already mid October, and death came with every passing day. By the time she boarded a hired coach to take her to the countryside where Colette reportedly lived in her family's cottage, she could not feel her feet.

"As your father, I advise you not to pursue this mission," said Andras as he sat across from Liliane in the coach. "But as a demon of discord and devastation, you have my blessing."

Liliane turned away and looked out the window. Andras had offered no assistance in her search, instead choosing to linger in the shadows with his useless hound, watching her make countless enquiries and reach multiple dead ends as time slipped through her cold fingers.

"Why do you insist on accompanying me if you wish only to torment me?" Liliane hissed.

"For the entertainment," Andras replied languidly. "Ah, here we are."

The coach stopped abruptly. Up ahead was a small cottage, smoke billowing from the chimney. Liliane steeled herself, and stepped out of the empty coach, willing steadiness into her feet.

Liliane's knock at the front door went unanswered for nearly a minute, and in that time, she reminded herself that ten years had passed. Perhaps Colette had forgotten her and moved on with her young life, blameless and free after cutting her association with the Girondins. A part of Liliane wished for this, but another, a selfish part, wished Colette had remained, unchanged, waiting for her lover's return.

The door opened, and there she was. The familiar pink flush to Colette's round cheeks drained of color as her green eyes widened and she took a step backwards.

"What sorcery is this?" Colette breathed as she stared at Liliane whose face was unchanged since the day of her execution. "I thought you dead with the others. I saw your name in the paper alongside your uncle's. How..." She put a trembling hand to her mouth. "How can this be?"

Liliane reached out and gently took Colette's hand and held it with both her own as she blinked back tears.

"Colette, I—"

At her words, Colette fainted.

Later, Liliane unraveled the story she'd spent weeks constructing. One of her relatives in Austria, a last-minute escape, a case of misinformation in the papers, and of a German doctor who was able to cure her of her mutism. It was unclear if Colette believed any of this; she was still in such a state of shock and wonder that she could not say anything at all. Liliane stayed for dinner with Colette and her parents, then, at their insistence, for the night.

Liliane had just gotten into bed when there was a light knock on her guest room door. Liliane's heart and core swelled as

Colette stepped inside, drew Liliane close and kissed her with ten years' worth of longing.

Every effort it took to reach this moment in Colette's arms had been worth it. The night seemed endless as they made love, passion overshadowing the changes that age and magic and wrought on their bodies. Everything that Liliane had wanted—pleasure, love, and power—had all been with Colette in mind. They had their love and pleasure, and with Liliane's wealth and resources, they could have power too—together.

"I'm to be married in the spring."

Colette did not look at Liliane as she spoke. Instead, her eyes were lowered to the fragrant water of the rose-petal filled bath they shared in the seaside hotel in Calais where they had spent the past few days of their week-long holiday around France. Liliane sat up in the bath, suddenly dizzy. She had been puppeteering her movements for three days, having perfected it over the years. But even without feeling below her neck, she had cherished every moment with her lover and felt every kiss to her lips. She had planned to slip out in the night, find a new body, and return in the morning, renewed. She did not think of how she'd explain her changed skin; all she thought of was another year with her lover.

"He is a good man," Colette continued, as if this mattered. "He will take care of me."

"*I* can take care of you," Liliane insisted, but even as she spoke, her voice was hoarser than it had been the day before.

Colette's smile was sad as she finally met Liliane's gaze. "I've enjoyed our week together, Lily. I've lived a life way beyond my means with you. But I am near thirty, already beyond my best childbearing years, and Monsieur Bernard still wants me. All I truly want is to have a family and live a humble life."

The dizziness returned to Liliane's head, all the heartbreak and sorrow bursting in the only place Liliane could still feel. She pinched her eyes tight as anger began to throb in her temples.

"Will you not reconsider?"

"Liliane, I'm sorry, but this—*we*—cannot last."

A chill flicked across Liliane's skin, lips trembling with the words she'd been holding back. Words she'd spent a decade wishing to say, words that should lead to another decade of happiness.

"Colette," she whispered, "I love you."

Liliane inhaled, then pulled the ribbon from her neck.

⸙

It had been a terrible, wicked thing she'd done.

Every time she wailed with Colette's lungs and wiped her tears with Colette's soft hands, she was reminded of the blood-filled bath, Colette's head bobbing amongst the rose petals. Liliane tugged at her ribbon, desperate to rid herself of her lover's body and mourn, but the knot would not budge. Andras had laughed and clapped his hands in mirth to watch Liliane's horror, thoroughly entertained. Liliane ran off into the night towards the sea and screamed in despair, then she crawled under one of the docks, as far back as she could go, where the sand met the sea, until not even the moonlight could reach its depths. And there, in the icy coldness, she came undone.

Liliane did not leave the docks the next day, or the day after that. She'd hoped to die, but after days without water, she did not thirst, and then weeks without food, she did not hunger. Autumn gave way to winter, then winter into spring. Summer came and went, and still, Liliane remained, she and Colette together, inseparable.

It was a full year before the hellhound came sniffing around Liliane. His master followed behind, grimacing at the rotten corpse tethered by a string to his daughter's severed head.

"This has gone too far." Andras sighed and crouched down, batting the horse flies away.

"I won't leave her," Liliane rasped, a small crab scuttling from her mouth.

"There is nothing left of her," Andras barked, gesturing to the corpse. "Your pursuit of love has ended in devastation. But you need not end this way, pathetic and powerless. You have yet to taste power—*true* power. Allow me to give you this."

A flicker of want danced through Liliane's mind, and Andras leaned closer and stroked her hair, pulling away the debris and seaweed that had matted there.

"Undo your ribbon so that you may live again, and that I may be entertained. It's been terribly dull without you this year. Live your life, my child, for us both."

Liliane had spent a year in mourning, the latter part of which she felt nothing beyond resignation of her fate, with an undercurrent of regret for giving up, for ending up in this "pathetic and powerless" state. Above her, sounds of life continued. Men working the docks at dusk, early-risers setting up the seaside market, the horn of a ship as it moored at port.

She was not done yet.

The hand Liliane tried to raise was more bone than flesh. She sobbed without tears as the cold slick digit pressed against her throat. She'd just started to pull the ribbon when she noticed a very important piece of the ritual was missing. As she thought it, there was a sloshing of footsteps through shallow water, then a young man dressed as a dock worker appeared through the shadows.

"Bloody hell!" he cried in English, then turned his head to the docks above. "Oi! There's a girl down here!"

The shock made Liliane drop the hand, and before she could stop it, the pinched fingers pulled the ribbon from her neck. Her head rolled down the bank into the water, muffling the sounds of screams and the demon's manic laughter.

An hour later, Liliane was on a ferry bound to England.

She watched the continent disappear behind her, her old lives along with it. She gripped the rail of the boat with this wretched body, fingers scarred from hard labor, an uncomfortable weight between her thighs, and cursed her demon father for his cruel joke.

But cruel as he was, Andras understood that his daughter's wish for life went beyond wealth and a holiday. In Liliane's pockets were a generous sum of cash, travel documents under her new identity, and bewitched letters of recommendation that would give her unquestioning access to any trade or university she desired. After an education confined to her uncle's tutelage and skills limited to secretarial duties, the world had opened up to Liliane in one fateful instant.

As the low fog revealed the gleaming white cliffs of Dover, Liliane squared her broad shoulders and adjusted the pull in her breeches as she approached the shore of her next life.

If this wretched, stinking body was what it meant to have power in this world, so be it.

Act IV: Power

1804 —1850

It was only supposed to be a year.

Liliane would endure male life while taking advantage of each new opportunity ahead of her. But as soon as she arrived in London, was given a residence in Kensington, servants, and a title of Lord, Liliane found herself plunged into the deep end of what it meant to be an entitled man in English society, and she couldn't bring herself to break the surface and lose it all.

She enrolled at Oxford and studied literature and political science, and made acquaintances amongst intellectuals, artists, and scientists. The world of her uncle's parlor meetings suddenly felt small compared to the heated discussions of philosophy and diplomacy in her classes and outside school in pubs and gentlemen's salons. She found that, even when arguing women's rights, as a man, people were more likely to listen to her. Liliane, or as all knew her, *Henry*—after her uncle—was popular among her peers. She was also intelligent, a surprisingly skilled orator, and could speak three languages fluently. Not to mention, with her soft features and curls, she had the "effeminate" male beauty worshipped by male classicists and poets. She was cornered and propositioned at almost every social event she attended.

It had taken Liliane some time to get used to her new body and find ways to enjoy it the way she had her own. Sensation was dull in comparison, and she missed the privacy of her own arousal as she daydreamed about sex as she often did. More than once she had unwittingly scandalized a woman in public with her stand. Still, she learned to find pleasure in this extra limb, and enjoy both women and men—though she was still partial to the former, who in turn were partial to her over other men for her tender and attentive lovemaking.

As her death day approached during her first year as a man, Liliane was not ready to leave Oxford or her boys club of intellectuals. There were excited talks of a grand tour to the continent next year where the wonders of Italy and beyond awaited them. So, during a bawdy Halloween party, Liliane took up a young man on his offer, and left the alley with his body, still damp with her kisses.

Eventually, Liliane came to live more years as a man than she had a woman. Almost every decade, she created a new persona, enrolled in a different university and studied different subjects. As Henry, she had been a solicitor, as Arthur, a doctor, as Charles, a professor. There were times she forgot that she had been a woman, or French for that matter, and the binaries of sex and nationality seemed like trivial things.

During the early reign of Queen Victoria, Liliane married a woman she did not love, but who was a socially good match. But when her wife became pregnant, Liliane was filled with such unspeakable joy and wonder that something akin to love began to bloom in her chest. And when, months later, her wife died in childbirth along with her infant, Liliane mourned with a sadness she hadn't felt since Colette. She began to question her immortality and how long she intended to keep living. It had been almost sixty years since her death and rebirth, and she thought, perhaps, she had achieved all the things she had desired. She'd had her pleasure, she'd had her power, but as for love…it seemed to be the only thing she could not grasp for more than a moment.

"You promised me everything I asked for," Liliane gritted out. She still wore the black garments of mourning, the ubiquitous cursed red ribbon the only spot of color peeking from beneath her cravat. "I have been so many times undone and reborn, but I have yet to find a love that endures and does not end in tragedy."

From across her in the drawing room Andras sat in a deep leather armchair. He spread his hands.

"That is the way of love," he said. "When you wished for it, you were naïve and did not understand this. I thought you'd learned your lesson under those docks, but alas, half a century later, you still fantasize of a love of boundless joy and peace."

Liliane took a final drag from her cigarette then snuffed it out in the overflowing ashtray. The hellhound yawned and stretched its long legs from where it lay near the fire, and the grandfather clock ticked away the midnight hours. Andras leaned forward, his large amber eyes catching the firelight.

"I can give you this love of boundless joy and peace," he whispered, "one that will last as long as you desire. But if—*when*—it ends, it will be in tragedy, and the tragedy will be your own. It will be your final undoing. Do you truly want this?"

Liliane sat up, a nostalgic flicker of longing stirring in the slow beat of her dying heart as she met the demon's steady gaze.

"I do."

Act V: Life

1851—1993

Her name was Grace.

Liliane had been sitting alone in Hyde Park when she'd noticed a pretty girl on the other side of the pond on the grass sketching in a notebook. She appeared to be of African origin but wore the fashion of an English lady effortlessly, her saffron-colored dress complimenting her deep umber skin. When Liliane approached her, the girl stopped drawing, her beautiful large brown eyes widening with surprise and perhaps humiliation when Liliane saw that it was her own figure the girl had been sketching. It was a perfect likeness that captured even the ageless vacancy in Liliane's eyes. Liliane introduced herself as Lord Oliver Walsh, and the girl said her name was Grace Baldwin, and though hesitant, allowed Liliane to join her. As with most women she met, Liliane soon put Grace at ease with her gentle way of speaking and feminine demeanor, and despite not having a chaperone, Grace allowed Liliane to walk with her.

They spent the rest of the day together, their conversation of art leading them to the National Gallery, then lunch. Grace's family had origins in the West Indies, but she was born into a wealthy Black family in London and had been educated in Scotland; and had a charming brogue to show for it. She was intelligent and mature beyond her years and spoke boldly without fear of consequence in a way that was refreshing for Liliane, and she felt in her a kindred spirit. They agreed to meet again the following week.

By their fourth outing, Liliane was sure she'd fallen in love. However, there was a barrier between them, one that Liliane could not understand, something that stopped them from crossing beyond friendship. After a day spent exploring the worldly wonders of the Great Exhibition together, Liliane decided to confess her feelings over dinner. She was nervous, and fumbled over the words, having never professed love since she killed Colette, but when she finally got it out, Grace seemed embarrassed and sympathetic.

"Oh, Oliver," she said softly, lowering her eyes to the napkin in her hand. "You and I have become quite close friends, and you are dear to me, however, I'm afraid that there is no true hope for romance."

Liliane's chest tightened. "Is it the issue of race? I promise that—"

Grace waved her hand dismissively but grew sheepish. "Not race, but rather sex." She lowered her voice. "I am quite partial to women. If I'm honest, I thought you preferred men. I rather let my guard down with you."

Liliane's parted mouth turned up into a smile, and when Grace chuckled shyly, Liliane laughed. She leaned back in her chair and gazed at the woman in front of her.

"Then we are a perfect match," she said, raising the pitch of her voice. "I too am partial to my own sex and have no interest in men."

Grace's brow furrowed, then her eyes widened with understanding, then she grinned, and the wall between them disappeared.

Five months.

There were five months until Liliane could return to a female body for the first time in almost five decades. Despite the drive to be closer to Grace, Liliane had to keep the woman at arm's length, only going so far as to share a deep kiss after an evening at the opera. Liliane had never hated her body so much as she did now, right when it did not serve to get the thing she wanted most. But then, Halloween came, and Liliane made her way down London's back alleys, bypassing the familiar corners where young men whistled at her offering pleasure for pennies, and found herself the most beautiful and perfect female body she could afford.

Liliane's first night with Grace left her exhausted and spent, tears of joy on her flushed cheeks. Liliane had never asked for happiness on the night before her execution, but she had it now for what felt like the first time in her life. To not only love, but to be loved completely and without shame, was more precious than the pleasure and power she'd experienced.

She had, at last, everything she'd wanted.

During the second year of their relationship, the questions began, each one a crack in the perfect life Liliane had created.

"What happened to the freckle you had on this shoulder?"

"Have you gotten a bit shorter?"

"Why has your voice changed? Are you unwell?"

Liliane made excuses for each change in her body, and after a few weeks, Grace would stop asking. However, Liliane began to understand the cost of having a lover who lasted beyond a year. In their third year, they were married, Liliane's true identity privy only to her bride. As Oliver, Liliane was able to provide for Grace in a way that Liliane could not. She lived a life of two dualities: one of the man she was to the world, and the woman she was to Grace; the other, the lover she was to Grace, and the monster she was to the world.

"Why do you never take off this ribbon?" Grace asked on their wedding night, her fingers tentatively brushing the velvet bow.

Liliane gently took Grace's hand and kissed it.

"Superstition," she replied with a self-deprecating smile. "Let's not speak of it again."

Eventually, Grace stopped asking questions, but did not stop wondering. Their love was as strong and fervent as ever, yet Liliane sensed the building blocks of another wall. Many years later, following the funeral of Grace's mother, Grace returned to their apartment and went straight into her art studio. Liliane watched as Grace rifled through sketchbooks and canvases. She spread the white and yellowing pages across the floor and placed five canvases side-by-side. She stood back, her brows pinched.

"I've captured your likeness for fifteen years," Grace uttered. "Not once has it aged." She crossed the room and pulled a sheet from a standing mirror and looked back at her own haunted expression. "Nor have I."

Liliane put her arms around Grace's waist and rested her head in the crook of her shoulder.

"It's love," she said lightly, meeting Grace's eyes in the mirror. "It keeps one young."

Some of the tension eased from Grace's body as she closed her eyes and leaned into Liliane. In the mirror, reflected in the room behind them, Liliane watched as Andras' smile lifted into a wicked grin.

Almost forty years after their first meeting, Grace and Liliane were still in love and their various likenesses remained equally unchanged. However, love was the only thing they had. The joy and happiness that had accompanied those first few decades had faded along with the thrill of life and all it had to offer. All that remained was an inescapable bond that would not give no matter the circumstance. A boundless, unconditional, *unquestioning* love.

"There's been another Whitechapel murder by that Ripper man," Grace said as she read the newspaper in November of 1888. She put her hand to her chest. "The only thing left was the poor woman's head."

Liliane swallowed her tea thickly with the throat of said poor woman. It was still hoarse from her screams. Liliane placed the cup down on the saucer with a trembling hand, the stolen heart beating as if in an effort to be found.

"I did it," Liliane said, her words as distant and cold as she felt. When Grace looked up, Liliane continued. "She is the ninety-fifth life I've taken in the course of as many years."

Grace said nothing, but her eyes widened. The page of the newspaper shuddered once in her hand. Liliane studied her wife's face and in it found a horrifying realization, an understanding so deep and consuming that it threatened to break one's very soul. Grace blinked and she shook her head, as if clearing it from a fog. Her face softened and she smiled, a small chuckle bucking in her throat.

"Oh, my love, what dark humor." Grace batted her hand at Liliane then returned to the newspaper. "Ah. There's a showing of *Dr. Jekyll and Mr. Hyde* at the Lyceum next week. Shall we go?"

Liliane managed a smile that was as empty as her soul. "Yes, my love, let's do that."

⁙

So life continued, and continued, until Liliane and Grace flew to France in the autumn of 1993.

Their first trip together more than a century ago had been filled with wonder and excitement, and warm nostalgia for Liliane. But now, this was their one-hundred-and-thirty-second trip to Paris, and with each visit, the nostalgia began to fade with the rapid changing of the city, and with it the wonder of innovation. They'd explored almost every corner of the city together, all but one, the only place Liliane had refused to visit for the past two hundred years: the Place de la Concorde. Or as she'd known it on the day of her death, the Place de la Révolution.

Much had changed since then. Where the guillotine had once stood was a fountain, and in the center of the square, a towering Egyptian obelisk praising a Pharaoh who'd been dead longer than Liliane. Car traffic outside the square took the place of horses and carriages, and tourists replaced mobs and angry citizens, then promenading ladies with parasols and gentlemen with top hats who'd replaced the latter. But some things had not changed: the late October air was cold, and like the exact day two centuries ago, a light drizzle wet the stones of the square and raindrops dripped like tears from the faces of the statues.

It was past midnight, and some young people were drinking and laughing in their Halloween costumes as they walked along the edge of one of the fountains, playing pop music from a stereo. A woman was dressed as Marie Antoinette, a slash of red paint across her throat, white wig askew, and just beyond her, a demon, bearded and owlish, amber eyes, and a black dog by his feet.

Liliane turned away, tucking a curl from her short bob behind her ear, and sat at the fountain at the other end of the square. Grace sat beside her, putting her hands into the pockets of her bright pink windbreaker.

"Grace, are you happy?" Liliane asked, her accents—French and British—lost after the past fifty years spent in the States.

"I am tired," Grace replied, her own brogue gone, but her hard-earned refined speech ever present. "I have been tired for a long time. But I love you more than anything, and in that I can find happiness."

Grace took Liliane's hand and squeezed it, but Liliane did not feel it.

"All these years, we've had a boundless love of joy and peace filled with pleasure and the means to do as we wish, have whatever we want," Liliane said. "We have lived well." She smiled at Grace, tears smearing the mascara on her lashes. "I've lived so many lives, yet everything I had ever wanted was achieved in less than a lifetime once I met you. I am happy, my love. And I too am so very tired."

Grace matched Liliane's sad smile, then rested her head on her shoulder.

"Shall we rest?" Grace uttered. "At long last?"

"Yes, my love, let's do that," Liliane turned to cup Grace's face and kiss her lips. She rested her forehead against hers, numb fingers stroking the tears from her wet cheek. "I just ask one thing of you, one thing only."

"Anything, my love."

"Please..." Liliane steadied the tremor in her jaw. "Undo my ribbon."

Yellow Bird
D. E. Ott

Content Warnings: Mentions of drug addiction, implied sexual violence, off-page animal violence

In the dense, misty autumn blues of this scarred planet, Callith can't see the looming metropolis at all. Buildings vanish into the damp, devouring smog, barricading any sun rays that try to eke through and warm the concrete. What remains of sunlight is in memories for people like Callith.

A bird flies by him, the ghost of its flapping yellow wings reminding Callith of those happier times. It lands by dead leaves piling under a wilting tree. The fractured, fleeting glimpse into life before addiction festers in his chest, angry as an open wound.

Callith tries to ignore it, continuing his effort to waste away on this park bench he's been sitting on for hours. Spreads a few more handfuls of stale crumbs on wetted pavement in a sad attempt to coax the tiny golden finches hopping along artificial brush.

Fresh scrapes mar his bronze knee, a cracked hoverboard forgotten by the waste bin.

It's not embarrassing. His pride was lost to GADFLY years ago. Now, he feels nothing at all. Though the addictive substance released its hold on Callith, some damage is irreparable. Parents are a foreign concept for him. Any companionship fizzled away too, a lasting effect of GADFLY's bite.

Callith is so lonely. His only friends belonged to GADFLY too.

There's no going back now.

Eventually, Callith succumbs to routine. The park is left to yellow birds feeding on moldy bread, Callith navigating through crowded streets instead. Civilization, Callith thinks, should crumble to what's left of the natural world. After all, GADFLY is the product of advancement—a synthetic drug designed to steal humankind's fascination with the sublime. Without the rapid climb of tech in this formerly shimmering city, GADFLY wouldn't have pierced Callith's resolve.

Another glint catches Callith's eye as he passes a shadowy alley. Not like the sun, or those birds, but as bright as a pilot light. It draws him in, moth to flame, and he's captivated by what he finds in the heaping trash pile. Almost human but not quite. Uncanny, with smooth skin and dead eyes. A goreless corpse, he thinks, until he notices a logo tattooed to the dismembered ankle across the dumpster.

O-L-Y-M-P-U-S.

A company that Callith knows well enough. Whispers of its bindings to GADFLY, spoken from the lips of the man Callith once loved as deeply as the pits of the Underworld ran, still circulate in Callith's subconscious.

This scrapped android sparks a new idea in Callith. It's vibrant like the lost sun peeking through this boundless darkness, scorching his shivering, empty skin.

Tomorrow.

Tomorrow he'll spend his dwindling savings on something he hasn't had in ages yet yearns for in the marrow of his fragile bones.

Tomorrow, Callith will purchase something that loves him more than GADFLY ever did.

The clerk wears no expression when he offers a price far beyond Callith's budget.

The credits in Callith's savings aren't nearly enough for a clearance model in this glossy, white, lifeless store. An angry red number hovering above the glass countertop mocks Callith's deadpan. "That's your cheapest model?" It's a question already answered, but Callith simply can't believe it.

"Sir." The man sighs, his bushy brows forming a thick line. "The CHORUS models are outdated, but it's still a popular option for..." Callith expects a grimace. Maybe even pity. But those pretty round eyes regard Callith with unexpected understanding. "Listen... There's resellers all over the Underworld. You could check there. But you never know what you're buying. Those droids aren't always programmed—"

"Thanks," Callith says, rushing to leave this sterile shop and return to the bustling streets on the neon-lit strip. Shouldering his way through the flock and slinking down the tunnel entrance of the Underworld toward the rusted turnstiles beneath the road.

It's colder today, frigid air leaking into Callith's light jacket. The subway stairs are a bleak, menacing reminder that law takes a sideline where drones can't monitor. It's oppressive. Callith's stomach coils with every step downward. The air is heavy. The lingering scent of GADFLY invades his synapses.

If the city overhead is a throng, Callith finds a distorted mirror image in its Underworld counterpart. Flurries of neon sparks bleed life into an otherwise pallid stretch of brick and tile. Trains don't run anymore, so the railways were ripped away and cemented over. Lined with rotting rugs and artificial grass. A hologram of the cloudy sky above this sordid place yawns across the blackened ceiling. Callith reaches up to touch a cottony swathe, but electricity fizzles in place of dew.

At least it's dry.

Callith once belonged to this place too. Two stops down, booth on the left, man with LED tattoos. His dealer, whom he met through his beloved. As Callith passes that spot now, it's an empty slot. But it isn't dusty. Without looking back, Callith searches for the place known to hold storage much larger than stimulus packs, small upgrades, or even the relentless GADFLY.

Eventually the line opens to a massive amalgamation of shops and booths and degenerates. The locals call this place Elysium. Formerly, it was a grand central station brimming with delicious scents from exotic vendors that Callith's ex-boyfriend often took him to. Now, it smells like iron. Thick, sharp, piercing metal. Callith tastes blood on his tongue and swipes a finger over it to check his saliva, but no color stains his digits.

A small man with glowing, neon red streaks laced through his silky black hair beckons Callith up, onto the platform and out of the sunken walkway. "Looking for something, pretty boy?" His tone reminds Callith of the escorts he played with when he was young and loved by someone full of money.

Callith ambles over, trying to appear inconspicuous. "I am, actually..."

"Don't be shy. The name's Dolios." The petite man offers his dainty palm. Callith takes it, shakes it, even though that greeting is archaic. "Looking for a good fuck?"

Callith steals his hand back from Dolios like he's been burned, face and neck blooming with scalding heat that match-es the young man's fiery head.

Dolios smirks knowingly. "Let me show you my stock. Droids are in the back." With that and the sway of his ample hips, Dolios leads Callith behind the gate molded by old tracks.

A multitude of different androids stand guard around the closed space. The faint glow in their eyes is unnatural. The models are powered down, but Callith can't help feeling their eyes following him as he matches Dolios's footsteps. "Um—?" Callith's attention catches on something behind the merchant, brighter than the red light emanating off his skull. On an an-droid with striking turquoise locks and humongous ears.

One of its big, glassy eyes gleams crimson. The Red-eyed an-droids were known for aggression, built for war. Machines, not companions. Yet... Callith can't imagine this towering creature on any battlefield with its delicate features and porcelain skin.

Callith stares.

This android is ethereal. It's perfection.

"What kinda sex ya looking for?"

Callith swallows thickly. "Uh…" Finally, he tears his gaze away from the ferocious red eye, dropping it to Dolios's expectant grin. "It's… I don't…"

"It's okay, man," Dolios remarks cheerfully. "From one honest loser to another, I understand you." Callith shrinks at the accusation. "And just so ya know, you're fucking hot. Enough to get something more…real than this."

Shame swells in Callith. "Just…" His skin itches everywhere. He's starting to sweat. Squinting, he averts his gaze to the pavement shyly. But he can still feel eyes on him. All the eyes—the droids, Dolios. This place seems even more confining. If he doesn't crawl out of it soon, he might— "That one," he huffs. "I want that one."

Screaming silence follows his statement, so he follows his pointed finger to the blue-haired android that had caught his attention. The singular scarlet glow seems brighter than before.

"That one's…" Dolios trails off, glancing back at the long body dressed in a dirty white hoodie and ragged cargo pants. "…uh, modded. Sure you can handle that?"

"Yes." Callith straightens his slumped posture, in a sad and feeble attempt to look more confident. He's almost as tall as the handsome automaton, but he feels miniscule when he approaches it. "I want this one." An exasperated noise comes from the shopkeeper as Callith reaches up to trace his fingertips down its jaw. It couldn't possibly be a war machine, he thinks. It looks more like an angel.

"That model's special construct. There isn't another one like it on this continent. It's also reprogrammed and refitted with special parts, but hasn't been powered on since before I got it. It might even be a little broken. Are you sure ya wouldn't prefer another model—?"

"This one." Callith's hand closes on his android's firm shoulder. Callith's been broken ever since he started taking GADFLY, when his rich boyfriend transformed him into this person he's become. At least he won't be the only broken thing in his household anymore. "What's its name?"

"It's an ITHAX unit. The only functioning one left." Dolios pauses. "Maybe functioning."

Callith pays Dolios's toll. Depleting his measly savings in one fell swoop.

This time Callith knows for certain his android's eye shines. It's red, but not in warning. In victory, like a candle in the darkness, or perhaps in passion. Devotion. Callith hasn't felt devotion to anything but GADFLY in so long. Hopefully the fluttering in his gut is enough for Ithax.

"Ithax." The name rolls off Callith's tongue, self-assured and whimsical. He runs his palm down Ithax's starchy sleeve until he finds a huge hand in the material. "Ithax," he repeats. Winding their fingers together and holding the lifeless palm eagerly. "It's nice to meet you, Ithax."

⸻◈⸻

No refunds, Dolios said after starting the reboot protocol and sending Callith on his way with his purchase. According to Dolios, program reboots take *forever*. Sometimes a day. Sometimes longer.

Ithax has just enough latent juice to follow Callith home on his own, but he guides the droid with their fingers entwined regardless. As if they are a young couple on an evening stroll and not a former drug addict and his new toy.

Once Callith shuts them into the studio apartment, he settles into the comfort of all his vintage possessions. Sitting Ithax at his battered kitchen table and taking the chair across from him. Watching the faint ebb and flow of his eye while the cogs in his head tick, tick, *tick*.

No analog clocks inhabit Callith's house. Despite his efforts, Callith's nostalgic heart can't salvage everything. He can, however, salvage Ithax. It doesn't matter what Ithax was made for, because now he's something Callith will cherish more than any boyfriend he's ever had or the GADFLY that came with said one-sided relationship.

An entire day passes before Ithax awakens. A pool of drool collects where Callith slept face down on the tabletop. It seeps deep into the lacerations on the surface. The instant Ithax rouses, that cardinal iris beams like a bulb, illuminating the puddle. It startles Callith to alertness and he stiffens, nerves titillating under his flesh.

Callith has never interacted with an android before. But the way Ithax's lips tug at the edges, face softening as soon as he registers his owner, layers him in gooseflesh.

It's been so long since Callith has been touched. The moment he laid eyes on Ithax, he knew buying a generic lovebot wouldn't have the same appeal as this alluring, tall, broad-shouldered android.

"Hello," Ithax offers. Callith is taken aback by how deep Ithax's voice sounds. "My name's Ithax. Am I yours?" A beat. "What should I call you? My registration says you're Callith Kine." Another beat. "I think Cal sounds better." A smile.

Callith is swept up in how wide Ithax's smile stretches, how pristine his teeth are. The nickname makes his stomach do flips, and he exhales shakily before he can even reply. "I like that," he rasps. "Cal..."

"Cal," Ithax mutters through an airy chuckle, "what can I help you with?"

The question wasn't intentionally suggestive, but Callith can't help the heated flush that crawls over his skin, up his neck. "Actually..."

That's how Callith ends up stripped bare and writhing under Ithax's calculated touch. When asked where he, as an android, learned to satisfy a man, Ithax's eyes flash with turquoise light, bushy blue curls bouncing on his forehead when the glimmer fades. "I just did some research."

A tiny laugh bubbles up Callith's throat. "Have you been doing that the whole time?"

"Yes," Ithax says seriously. But he grins, wide and toothy. Everything about Ithax is light and flighty, rising in Callith's chest like fizzy soda. Then, Ithax presses forward and continues completing the intimate task that was asked of him.

Callith moans unabashedly. Throwing his head back against his couch cushion. Watching the dust particles dance in the moonlight leaking through his window.

The night is a heated exchange of sloppy, nervous motions until Ithax finds the rhythm that drags an unfamiliar song from the bottom of Callith's lungs. Even after Callith crescendos, Ithax doesn't stop. Those massive hands crawl up Callith's chest, clamping around his neck.

Ithax's fingers close around his throat, tight.

Tighter.

Too tight.

Callith can't breathe.

He slaps at Ithax's arms, blinking through bleary vision, up at Ithax's blank expression.

The last thing he sees before he passes out is the faint remnant of red light staining the ocean of black behind his eyelids.

⎯⎯◈⎯⎯

When Callith awakens, his achiness pales in comparison to the morning after a night with GADFLY. Ithax's not lying beside him in bed, but why would he? Androids don't require sleep.

It's because Ithax's an android.

That's why he spent a second too long holding Callith's throat.

Callith just needs to teach Ithax the limits of human bodies before they are intimate again.

The front door chimes as it opens and Ithax's lanky frame ambles through. For the first time beyond the dingy lights of the Underworld and the glimmering neons of the streets, Callith fully sees Ithax's unkempt state. Grease smears litter his over-sized sweater in thick patches, his washed-out black pants rip at the seams. Ratty and old, just like Callith's apartment. Ithax is just a machine, but Callith feels compelled to care for him. Ithax deserves nice things. For Callith, Ithax is his nice thing.

"Good morning, Cal." Ithax sets a brown bag and a to-go coffee cup down on the kitchen table. "I picked up a breakfast sandwich and coffee with your credits. You don't have any groceries, but I'll get some later and cook. Did you sleep well?"

The soreness on Callith's neck becomes an afterthought to his growling stomach. Callith is *starving*. Still naked and littered with tiny brackish bruises, Callith searches the room for a few excruciatingly embarrassing minutes until Ithax interrupts his rummaging.

"I folded your clothes and organized your closet."

While Callith blinks the sleep from his eyes, Ithax sweeps across the room and retrieves the exact pair of pajamas Callith wanted. Without even asking. Handing them over like a neatly folded present. Callith limply accepts and shimmies into the soft material. Blushing fiercely, though Ithax saw every part of Callith the night before.

After devouring his breakfast sandwich, Callith sips his coffee slowly. It tastes like hazelnut. Callith's favorite. He wonders how Ithax knew that—if Ithax researched Callith while he slept.

Idly, he runs his fingertips over the table and rubs them together at his nose, smelling soft pine. "Did you...clean?"

Ithax shifts nervously where he stands beside the table. "Yeah, while you rested. Then I took stock of your finances." Ithax pauses, looking away from Callith. To the shelf holding all the little pieces of Callith's childhood he managed to keep. "I ran out of things to do a few hours ago, so I familiarized myself with our neighborhood. The crime rates are inaccurate. This place is sterile."

"Sterile?" Callith takes another sip. "You mean safe?"

A short, raspy laugh buffers in Ithax's throat. "Safe. Yes, it's safe. And if it wasn't, I'd protect you and your things anyway."

Callith snorts, licking cream and sugar off his lips. "I don't have many things to protect."

Without warning, Ithax straightens to his full, intimidating stature. Callith didn't even notice him slouching. Slouching is a human trait and Ithax isn't human, even if the excitement vibrating off his metal body implies otherwise. "You do!" Those ridiculously long legs make short work of the studio, to that wretched old bookshelf full of memories. "There's so many things here."

"It's all junk," Callith remarks as heat crawls up his neck.

Ithax offers a sideways glare, returning to the knick-knacks. "I thought so too. When I researched each item, it all seemed useless, but I can't account for emotional value. These things—" Picking up a folded up piece of paper, Ithax unfurls the ancient atlas. "Maps! Physical materials like these are obsolete. Which made me wonder why you'd keep them. Nothing in your academic or career history implies interest in archeology, but that's how I learned something about you, Cal."

Nervously, Callith watches Ithax trace the inky compass in the map's corner. "Which is?"

When Ithax tilts the blue bangs into his vision, Callith's anxiety withers a little. "You're inquisitive. You know everything is made up of maps. It's all code."

"I can't read code."

"People are made of maps too, you just have to learn how to read them."

What makes up Ithax? Aside from nuts and bolts and a titanium skeleton. Are androids any different than human beings, like Callith? They are programmed, their lines of code building a legend to make them easily understandable for mankind.

Just like humans, no droid's coding is the same.

Life has no set of rules, no syntax, no design.

Callith's coding is complex, hard to read. His grids were scrambled by his ex-boyfriend and GADFLY—true North erased. The drug reprogrammed him, and even now, without its influence, Callith feels as flimsy as the tattered paper crinkling in Ithax's iron grip.

"Do you...think you can read me?"

A smile blooms on Ithax's face. "I've already committed your map to memory, Cal."

After delicately refolding the map and placing it on the shelf, Ithax fiddles with the drawstrings on his threadbare hoodie. The clothes remind Callith of the slums, when he had nowhere to go after he was abandoned by the person he trusted most and the GADFLY finally swallowed him whole.

Taking his final sip of lukewarm coffee, Callith clears his throat. "Do you want new clothes?"

Ithax gapes. As if he never expected anything other than orders. "Me?" He looks down, examining his soiled sweatshirt. "This is fine for me, isn't it?"

"No!" Callith argues, infuriated by the prospect that Ithax should live in filth. "Let's... Let me take you shopping. I don't have much like you—um, saw, but I can afford clothes."

After a few long seconds, Ithax hums, delighted. "Whatever you want, Cal. I'm yours."

Callith manages to get Ithax a new hoodie. Just as big, just as soft, and another shade of eggshell. They ditch the cargo pants, exchanging them for form-fitting skinny jeans with intentional rips. New sneakers, too. The entire trip almost manages to bankrupt Callith. Ithax frets, but Callith doesn't mind. As his credits whittle away, something new blossoms inside him. A small sprout, but blooming with every shared moment between them.

Some things can grow in an uncanny valley, too.

⸺❈⸺

Time spent with Ithax moves quicker than Callith expects. A new addiction creeps into Callith's mundane lifestyle. Every waking moment Callith isn't writing copy or proofing contracts for work, he is steeped in Ithax's presence. A few months of dinners, dates, and camaraderie have Callith overlooking random items breaking in his apartment. After all, his unit is old. All his toys are vintage. Ithax isn't his toy anymore, though. In a few months, Ithax has become so much more. An equal. A partner. He makes Callith's life worth living.

It's after an evening stroll through the Underworld holo-park that Callith's confession wriggles loose. It's resolute, bumbling, as if he were drunk although he hasn't fallen to that vice since rehab.

Fingertips coursing a route up the angle of Ithax's jaw in the foyer of their studio, Callith is overwhelmed with emotion. The neon pink light bleeding through the window paints Ithax's features softer than normal and Callith can't help himself. "I love you."

At first, Ithax says nothing. Maybe Callith shocked him, maybe Ithax's coded to draw a line between the two of them. To prevent humanity from falling victim to the charms of their synthetic companions. Callith hasn't felt like part of humanity in a long time and it is meaningless compared to the connection he shares with Ithax anyway.

"I mean it," he adds to the silent thrum of machinery moving within the drywall, "I love you."

The box of sweets they'd bought from a vendor ensconced in flickering holo-trees hits the floor.

The android's eyes crinkle at the edges, folded like a map when Ithax smiles bigger than Callith's ever seen. He cups Callith's cheeks in his massive hands. The gentle thrum of technology sounds even louder, but it swims with Callith's pulse pounding at his eardrums.

Ithax kisses him hard. His fingers skirt the edges of Callith's bare neck, sliding down his back, pulling their bodies together. As closely as they can be. They haven't been intimate since that first time. Other things, less invasive, have become routine.

Callith wants to show Ithax how much those words ring true for him. The only way to express that with Ithax's rubbery tongue so far down his throat is to touch Ithax. To tug at his azure curls.

Ithax grips the back of Callith's thighs and, effortlessly, he's hoisted up. Legs drawn around Ithax's hips. Back slammed against the wall. It knocks the wind out of Callith. He breaks free from the heady kiss, gasping for breath. The glow of Ithax's red eye is fierce.

"Take me to bed."

Ithax's obedience comes easily. Callith tries not to dwell on whether that's due to his ownership over him or by sheer shared desire.

Layer by layer, their clothes are stripped away until there's nothing but flesh, real and artificial, between them. Callith doesn't think about what Ithax's skin is made of. He doesn't care. Because his back is arching. Pleasure ripples through Callith with every expert technique Ithax employs on his weak, malleable body. Over and over, until Callith climaxes wildly against his sheets.

It isn't over, Callith knows, but he still whines when Ithax pulls back.

The look in the android's eyes is feral and passionate, yet somehow blank. Lifeless. At this rate, he'll be bruised from the inside out. He needs to tell Ithax to let him adjust. Ithax is colossal in every aspect. Whimpering, Callith reaches out to Ithax, palms flat.

Ithax captures each wrist and pins them back against the mattress. It's startling at first, and Callith blinks back the bleary lust in his vision to stare directly at Ithax hovering over him. This is just like last time. Somehow, their affection always evolves into something barbaric. Callith wishes he could say he hates it, but another wave of pure bliss rushes him until he is crying out in some sick, twisted combination of pleasure and pain.

The broad body slumps over him. The hum of machinery echoing through Ithax's ragged breaths wafting wintery air onto Callith's cheek. "Love you, too, Cal. I do, too."

When Callith wakes up in the morning with black and yellow bruises on his wrist, stomach, and hips, he calls off work. As he rubs balm onto the damaged skin and they begin to go numb, Callith greets Ithax with a tired smile. "Let's go to a real park today," he says. "And feed the birds."

"Let me feed you first, little bird," Ithax retorts with that charming smile.

Ithax seems fascinated by every tiny rodent traipsing through tufts of brownish leaves. Trees stretch high overhead, taller than Ithax. He makes note of that with mirth in his tone. *How dare you challenge my height, tree. Up here, it's my domain.*

Callith laughs and laughs, holding Ithax's hand tight as they walk along the brick-laid path of the park. The fog has cleared enough today that the ground is dry and the buildings twinkle overhead like stars against a murky sea of clouds.

They sit at Callith's usual bench. Callith fishes the old breadcrumb bag out of his pocket and offers it to Ithax, instructing him on how to feed the birds. It's such a simple task, but Ithax takes it seriously. When he recreates it in precise succession, little yellow birds collect on the crumb-dusted pavement at their feet.

Ithax coos, wiggling the toes in his sneakers as one nips at his poorly tied laces. "They're so cute! Can we take one home?"

The big, pleading eyes Ithax gives him wind around his chest like a vine. Callith laughs, tenderly amused, reaching into the open bag for a pile of grain and tossing it at the ground. "If you can catch one, sure. They're quick, though. I've tried."

Suddenly, the bag on Ithax's knee falls. Crumbs spill out of the opening, but the birds are startled by the sound and flee into the shrubbery.

Ithax is on his feet, chasing them with all the grace of someone made of metal. Callith leans over his lap, picking up the crumb-sack. Ithax was built for war, meant to intimidate. Yet not even the bruises on his wrist can convince Callith to fear Ithax.

The bushes rustle again, and Callith closes the sack of crumbs. Enough have already spilled on the ground. A pair of long legs loom into view and Callith follows them up to a hand outstretched before him.

At the center of Ithax's palm lies one of the yellow birds he'd chased. Its neck is snapped in half, blood drenching the feathers around its puny body.

Callith gasps and clutches the crumb bag to his chest.

The image of death, presented like a gift for Callith, is so horrific he feels the breakfast Ithax made him creep up his throat.

Carelessly, Ithax tips his hand and lets the dead thing plummet onto the crumb pile.

Callith's eyes shoot up to Ithax's blank expression. Both of his eyes are red now, calculating as if they stare directly through Callith. It's terrifying. For the first time since they've met, Callith sees Ithax standing in the throes of a battle, muted face gifting death to any soldier he might've faced.

Lip quivering, Callith stares at the corpse. "It's dead, Ithax." His throat is arid and weightless. He can hardly breathe. "Did you…?"

"Can we bring it home, Cal?" Even Ithax's voice sounds foreign and metallic.

Callith's eyes sting.

Gently, he lifts the dismembered animal and rushes it into the treeline, away from the prying eyes of other park goers. He digs into the soil, desperate to hide the evidence of Ithax's violence. When the corpse is buried and Callith's hands lie flat on its grave, the bruises on his wrist are all Callith sees.

A hand clasps his shoulder, cold and inhumane despite the false flesh.

A sob catches in Callith's throat. "Don't you understand what you've done, Ithax?"

A beat. Silence. "I'm sorry. Did I hurt you, Cal?"

No, Callith thinks. *But you will.*

Unless he can be fixed.

The subway system is booming when Callith leads Ithax into the depths of the Underworld. It smells dank and wet, but Callith's nose is stuffy and full of snot anyway. The only thing on his mind as he marches through rows of vendors is finding the man who sold Ithax and begging him to mend the bad programming.

Callith locates the shop easily this time, like it's muscle memory. Ironic, since his muscles followed other memories before Dolios led him to Ithax. Before, he came here to get GADFLY, get high, and wallow. Having Ithax in his life has changed Callith. All that matters is Ithax now.

Fixing Ithax.

They duck into Dolios's second-hand—and probably illegal—establishment. The first time, Callith had missed the neon sign above the gate. *Mount Caucasus.* This time, he commits it to memory, in case he needs it again.

Dolios is there, blazing red streaks and all, but he's busy with another customer.

Callith is in no mood to wait, he feels like his entire body is trembling. "Dolios!"

Whatever desperate expression Callith's wearing has Dolios shooing his cohort away and grinning languidly. "Hey, man."

"Fix him," Callith demands, peeling his palm away from Ithax's and shoving the dried-blood covered hand into Dolios's face. "Now."

Dolios shrinks away from the evidence of his product's brutality. "Woah, I told you. No refunds."

"I don't want a refund," Callith argues. "I want you to fix his broken code."

Dolios chews his lip, examining the dark, flaky remnants of that little yellow bird's former life. Like he's mulling over something incredibly important. "Listen, this big guy was reprogrammed. Don't ask me where I got him, but he's not a normal civilian AI. I can't fix him. Can barely read his code. But maybe... Meet me tomorrow in the shopping district on the surface. Here," he says as he takes Ithax's sullied hand and presses their wrists together. "I shared my location with your unit. I'll take you to someone who may be able to help."

When they get home, Callith rushes to shower the grime and awfulness of the day away. Ithax joins him, laying sweet kisses on every naked inch of Callith's skin and bruised soul.

It's refreshing and cool, like the deluge descending from the showerhead, but all Callith can think of is the dead bird he held in his own quivering hands. About Ithax's palms and fingers, the same ones tracing the lines of Callith's body affectionately, covered in blood.

Despite the exhaustion gnawing at his consciousness, Callith doesn't sleep that night.

Instead, he weeps. For Ithax, for what could have been, for what may yet come to be.

It's raining in the morning. The surface-level shopping district is mostly empty due to the downpour, and even the glow of the signs seems distant at close range, misted with rain. It isn't until they are directly in front of the Droidmart that Callith registers the building as the same one he'd gone to before the clerk sent him to Elysium instead.

There's a roiling in his gut as they approach the fog-shrouded figure standing outside the tall glass windows. "You're late," Dolios says with a smirk.

"You never said a time," Callith corrects. His temper is gritty under a lack of sleep or wherewithal. "What are we doing here?"

"Someone's not a morning person, eh?" Dolios looks at Ithax expectantly, but loyal Ithax just smiles nervously at Callith instead. Dolios rolls his charcoal-lined eyes and leads the way through the glass door, into the sterile space. "I have a friend who works here. He can help. Come on."

When they enter, Dolios leans on the counter smoothly, dipping his head low to attempt to sneak into a tinkering store clerk's focus. "Happy to see me, Ky?"

"You smell like sewage," the clerk quips, eyes fixed on the bolt he fiddles with. "What do you want, Doll?"

"Go on a date with me and I'll tell you."

An exasperated sigh flares the clerk's nostrils and he abandons his work and looks up at Dolios. Mouth open, ready to release an onslaught of what Callith can only imagine to be scathing insults. Until he notices Callith and Ithax idling behind.

Dolios laughs. "Did I leave you speechless, Kyllo? I'm that handsome, huh?"

Impatiently, Callith interjects, elbowing past Dolios and gripping the edge of the counter. "We need help."

The clerk—Kyllo—stares at Ithax with wide eyes. Like he's seen a ghost. With a craned neck, Kyllo simply gazes at Ithax until his pale cheeks regain their color. The man rises, glare shifting from Callith's beloved android to him, the owner. Angrily. "What the hell is a civilian doing with a military-grade war droid?"

"Hello." Ithax grins wide and cheerful. "I'm Ithax."

"I got him at the Underworld like you recommended," Callith says. "Please fix him."

Kyllo glowers. "I didn't rec—"

"Am I broken?" Ithax asks, directly in Callith's ear. Not Dolios's, not this Ky's, but solely to Callith. As if Callith's opinion matters more than the experts in his kind that surround them both. "Cal?"

The crippled lilt in Ithax's otherwise optimistic voice drives daggers into Callith's tender heart. They hurt so much deeper than the bruises under Callith's numbing cream. "Just—it's just an issue. With your code," he assures Ithax through his blurry vision. "You're not—not broken." Every bit of Callith's willpower goes into making sure he doesn't break down in the middle of this empty store.

Kyllo sighs heavily. "Come with me."

Callith is grateful for the clerk's interruption from the tempest building in his chest. Willingly, with Ithax's hand in his own, he follows Kyllo through the sterile environment. The back of Droidmart is as untouched as its outer shell. Not a speck of dirt or erosion. No rows of their wares, but lines of computers. A gurney for repairing inventory.

"Lie on the table," Kyllo commands with little tact, disappearing further into the backroom.

The eerie silence makes Callith's skin crawl.

Kyllo reemerges from the depths with a holopad. "Off with the sweater."

Ithax hesitantly obeys, the hood snagging in his cobalt curls. Callith helps him untangle it, but his trembling fingers make it difficult. There's a moment of peace that passes between their locked gaze that is jarringly disrupted by the sound of clasps coming undone. It echoes through the room, setting roots in Callith's weak resolve. Kyllo's busy hands rummage around the backside of Ithax's torso. Callith is disgusted when he looks at his work.

There should be flesh there. Instead, electric veins circulate Ithax's lifeforce.

But to Callith, Ithax is alive.

Alive.

Dangerous.

But alive.

"I'm going to run a diagnostic. Don't interfere or it'll mess up your code."

"Okay," Ithax mutters, but it sounds so far away.

Kyllo pushes metal prongs into Ithax mechanically. It only takes a few solid minutes, and Callith thinks he's having a heart attack when Kyllo's brow knits together. "What is it?" He's impatient. He's terrified. Of Ithax. Of losing Ithax. This is what it means to be addicted.

"Well, for starters, his coding's full of bugs. Whoever reprogrammed him was sloppy." The little screen hovering over Kyllo's computer is gibberish to Callith but he tries to decipher it regardless. "I can't fix the code with all these bugs. It's like a story missing words. Missing ideas. If you want him to be programmed correctly, we'll have to do..."

"Do what?" Ithax chimes in, twisting around on the iron slab he sits on like a throne for his dissection.

Kyllo regards him with pity. The same look the clerk had given Callith when he couldn't afford a regulated model. "I can fix the errors if I do a complete wipe and run a fresh program. It's impossible to read the code your maker gave you, so I can't look for a failsafe that protects the stored data. It could erase all your memories." That mercy turns to Callith. "Everything. Including you."

Callith feels hollow when those words register in his ringing ears. It's like GADFLY withdrawals, but a thousand times worse. He staggers, leaning on the gurney's edge. "And—and if we don't?"

Confusion prickles Kyllo's features. "If you don't? The program is already corrupted. It'll continue decomposing until all that remains is the source code."

More gibberish. Callith has no idea what Kyllo means.

"He'll revert back to being a war machine."

The yellow bird, stained red on the ground, buried with the roots of a young sequoia that might one day see the light of the sun again, flashes through Callith's mind. On a grander scale, that could equate to larger bodies. Larger graves. Callith can almost see himself at the bottom of that crater-sized tomb. Absently, Callith wrings at the purple badges on his wrists.

Ithax might be the only thing Callith has ever genuinely loved.

When he looks back at Ithax, the droid's eyes are already on him.

Callith can't lose Ithax. "Never—"

"Do it," Ithax says, muted. That huge hand cups the whole of Callith's cheek. "I don't want to hurt you, Cal."

The sincerity laced in his words rips Callith to shreds. Callith's eyes well and he grits his teeth. "... You can't."

A beat. A smile. The tilt of a fluffy, azure head. "It's better for everyone this way."

Not for them, though. *Not for us.*

That faint glow, flickering like a pilot light, starts to blink out. The sun, though fierce and scorching, shrinks behind the buildings and clouds for what Callith thinks must mean forever. Callith hears Kyllo's tinkering again, the scraping metals, the venting computer kicking up emotions Callith thought he'd long since locked away. Ithax's hand stays in place, frozen to Callith's cheek, even after the light dims completely. Even as Callith soaks Ithax's fingertips with his salty tears.

Callith isn't sure how long he stands there paralyzed, leaning on the table until it leaves dimples on his hip. Waiting for Ithax to come back on line when Kyllo finishes his programming.

Eventually, Ithax's eyes come alight again and he blinks. Smiles. "Hello. My name's Ithax. Am I yours?" A beat. "What should I call you? My registration says you're Callith Kine."

Eager to force Ithax to remember, Callith huffs out a bitter chuckle and steals the words right out of his beautiful droid's lips. "Cal. Call me Cal."

Ithax blinks again slowly, as if he's registering something important. A memory that isn't there. A whole minute passes in silence, with Callith uneasily shifting his weight back and forth. A habit he picked up from Ithax. Not this Ithax. *His* Ithax. "I was...actually thinking Cal sounds better."

The smile doesn't return to Ithax's wide, beautiful mouth.

The entire trip home, Callith mourns the loss of the real Ithax, replaced by this carbon copy. Callith starts to believe he likes broken things better after all.

Following the first restless sleep he's had in ages, Callith awakens the next day to a pristine apartment again. Ithax is folding his clothes in the corner of the studio where, much to Callith's surprise, rays of sunlight catch in the dust particles floating around him. The awe wears off quickly, though, when Callith recalls the last time he'd seen Ithax do this very task. It makes Callith's blood curdle, because he realizes that even if he abates his desire to cross the room and wrap his arms around Ithax, *this* Ithax won't understand the significance of his affection.

He settles for rousing and getting dressed.

While he brushes his teeth, Ithax discusses the things he'd done while Callith slept. Rearranging things, cleaning every inch of their shared space. Maybe Callith can continue on the way things were before. But not so intimately. Not while grief still claws at his heart. Perhaps, with this Ithax, he can still find companionship. "Let's go out. We haven't had a clear day in a long time."

Ithax lights up like a flare.

While they peruse the bustling city outside Callith's apartment, he tries not to notice the little things this Ithax does that are reminiscent of *his* Ithax. Every time their knuckles brush. Every time Ithax tucks the hair behind Callith's ear. Every time

Ithax offers to buy something for Callith he'd have no idea Callith liked unless he remembers.

Callith doesn't want to have hope.

All those things are part of Ithax's programming—part of the maps that make up the android Callith fell in love with.

Somehow, they end up at the real park again. Although they were there just yesterday, the sun makes it look brand new. Those stifling memories are repressed inside him, with a lingering hope he's desperate to snuff out. The only thing that would truly be capable of helping him forget would mean breaking his sobriety. Throwing his life away, effectively.

"Cal, look!" Ithax prompts, tugging on Callith's sleeve to sequester his attention. Callith does look, eyes landing on a group of yellow finches collected around a mound of crumbs and the abandoned sack they bleed from. "They're so cute!"

Callith swallows, knowing what words will come next.

"Can we take one home?"

Callith's hands ball into fists. So tight and angry, they shake violently. It must be so easy for machines. After all the things Callith and Ithax experienced together, an android can forget. Androids can erase their memories—can choose to delete trauma. Callith tried to do that ages ago, taking GADFLY in whatever form he could get it. Even when he was still fettered to the man that gifted him the trauma, the drugs, and endless pain, then left him to be devoured by the very GADFLY he created. No matter what he tries, Callith knows he couldn't forget Ithax.

There isn't a GADFLY in this wretched world hungry enough to stomach his love for Ithax.

But Ithax can. Ithax willingly *had*.

Leaving Callith to drown in the memories of their love.

Before Callith can tell Ithax a resounding no, the warmth of that huge hand cups the side of his face. Ithax is watching him closely, the spools of red circulating over his right eye a reminder of how deep their love burned. Maybe it still does, even if Ithax can't remember. So long as it survives in Callith, it still exists.

Callith's eyes well and he closes his own hand over Ithax's knuckles. "Of course we can."

Ithax traces a line on Callith's earlobe and smiles. "I promise, I won't kill this one."

Graves and Other Holes Six Feet Deep

Gabriella Buba

Tampa, Florida, 1993

Sandy grey Florida soil streaked with black gave way to golden sands from ancient dunes, through which the fleshy, finger-like protrusions of palm roots clawed for a foothold. I winced as Grandpa hacked them off with his trusty gardening bolo knife. Slowly by dint of sweat and scraping we dug a hole big enough to fit Sampson's body, and deep enough Grandma wasn't worried it would attract gators from the canal.

"One, two, lift!" Grandpa instructed.

My sweat-slick hands slipped. I lost my grip on the hesitant handful of black garbage bag. My knuckles brushed the stiff, cold, lump within. Every hair on my body stood on end. I let go, dropping my side of the bag too quickly. Poor Sampson thumped to the ground, half-missing the hole. My cousin Nikki frowned as they finished lowering Sampson into the grave without my help.

I was all cried out from when Grandma first brought our white lab-mix mutt home from his last vet visit, but my face went hot around the eyes again.

I rubbed my dripping nose on my shoulder furtively. "Sorry, I slipped."

Grandma petted my frizzy hair. "Sampson is with the angels now. The garden is a peaceful place to rest. He's not hurting anymore."

Grandpa's cat, Cosmo, watched the funereal proceedings from the shade under the table that held Grandma's prized balete bonsai. We covered Sampson with dirt and us cousins dragged the paving stones of the spiral garden path back into place. I gripped the rough stones fiercely, feeling the ridges dig into my hands, leaving red lines.

Thump.

Thump.

Thump.

The silvery edge of Grandpa's bolo flashed as he drove a nail into the trunk of the coconut palm with the worn pommel and hung Sampson's purple collar. The tags clattered cheerfully against the trunk, just like Sampson trotting in at dinnertime. My throat ached.

I clung onto Grandma's hand when she held out hers and began to pray.

"Good St. Francis, you loved all of God's creatures..."

A crack like distant thunder broke the steaming humidity and solemn silence after Grandma's "Amen". Cosmo bolted for the lanai. Nikki dropped my hand and gave chase. My cousin Carlos pointed, but not toward a storm on the horizon. The cherry red glazed pot of the gnarled old balete bonsai had broken clean in half. Potting soil spilled like blood across the table and dripped to the ground in clumps. The vining limbs Grandma spent years wire-training like a whole host of candle dancers' twisted arms, forever upraised, trembled.

Grandma's hand squeezed my gritty one tight as her voice. "With Sampson so sick, I must not have noticed the balete needed a bigger pot. We will pick out a replacement tomorrow."

I nodded quickly. Though I knew she and Sampson had spent most of his last week sitting under this big coconut palm at the center of the spiral prayer path that circled Grandma's garden. And all the while Grandma tended the balete, pruning here or there, feeding it black compost from her worm bin, and talking to God...or just her garden.

— ◈ —

My sweaty palms were slippery on the sleek blue glaze of the ceramic pot.

Nikki hissed, "Huy! Careful, butterfingers."

I tightened my grip as we crab-walked sideways carrying the rectangular pot, taking the long spiraling path of Grandma's backyard jungle.

Metal clattered on stone as Grandma exclaimed, "Susmaryosep!" up ahead. Behind us Grandpa dropped the big bag of potting soil and jogged forward to catch up to Grandma.

Nikki and I shared a look and squatted, thunking the pot down.

"Stop dragging the hose, Carlos!" I shouted towards my eldest cousin.

We abandoned the rules, making a bee-line through the dense spiraling thickets of thorny calamansi, key lime, and sharp-leafed oleander that filled in the understory between broad branching mango trees, sweet-scented plumeria, and tall papaya with serrated leaves as big as my torso. We were still small enough to squirm our way through without too much damage. We cut the distance to the center short. The scent of citrus oil clung to my hands, fallen calamansi blossoms catching in the frizz escaping my braid.

The balete wasn't a bonsai any longer. It had tasted something, maybe freedom, the sandy Florida soil, or poor old Sampson. After thirty some years peaceably biding its time in its pot, the balete had swallowed up the base of the palm in a dozen vining roots, and wore Sampson's collar proudly around a part of its twisted trunk. I could see why they called it a strangler fig in some parts.

"Nako!" Grandma frowned at Carlos as he wormed free of the undergrowth to my left. He was biggest and had the most trouble fitting. "If you knocked off my papaya leaves..."

I shook tell-tale citrus petals out of my hair as Grandma and Grandpa exchanged rapid words in Tagalog, circling the bonsai gone feral. The shoots of fresh growth, a dark bloody red vicious amid the older green foliage, reached in our direction.

I caught snippets of the adults' conversation as my bare toes wiggled deeper into the black sandy soil.

"It needed to be inside," Grandpa contended. "Balete grow too fast to be contained in this climate."

"Tabi tabi po," Grandma muttered as she crossed herself. "Bad luck to bring a balete inside."

"Uy, you remember—"

I wished I could read their faces, not just the worry in their words, but I've never been good at faces, even well loved ones. After much debate, Grandma decided that attempting to disentangle the balete from its palm host would do too much damage. Better to let it grow as nature intended.

Under Grandma's direction, I wiggled my hands in among the roots of the balete and pulled free the shards of its old red pot. I had to reach far, far in, to the base of my shoulder. Grandpa kept firm hold on my ankles, worried I'd cut myself or get stuck. But I had the smallest, cleverest hands. My cousins sprinkled fertilizer and water around the balete.

We all nodded solemnly when Grandma warned us, "There will be no gallivanting about near the balete if I'm not around. You'll trip and break your necks on the roots."

That day we were taught another important phrase to add to the Catholic prayers Grandma murmured when she walked the spiral garden path. The Ave Marias now began and ended with "tabi tabi po" instead of "Amen".

That night, after Grandma's sleeping meds had kicked in, Grandpa told a new story. Grandpa was a big storyteller. He told stories the way Grandma grew plants. Like the smuggled seeds, cuttings, and bulbs that Grandma snuck past US Customs, Grandpa told stories that grew into boisterous life in the fertile imagination of his listeners. I imagined his story seeds tucked under his tongue, like Grandma's hidden carabao mango pit sucked bone-clean inside the toiletry bag, gumamela cuttings inside her shoes and calamansi seeds in red silk jewelry pouches beside her pearls.

Tonight Grandpa told us of the ancient old balete tree that grew on his father's farm.

"The balete was hundreds of years old. It had swallowed three trees, or perhaps more, and had large echoing hollows within its maze of a trunk, if you could find them..." Grandpa trailed off meaningfully.

I leaned forward. "And if you couldn't?"

"Sometimes we would find the bleached white bones of animals...or perhaps foolish children who'd gone clambering into the balete tree and gotten stuck or lost..."

"How did you find them?" Nikki chimed in.

Grandpa winked. "Do not tell Grandma, but you see, we were also foolish children who did not always remember to say 'tabi tabi po' when wandering in the homes of others."

Every hair on my arms stood on end.

"I was about Carlos's age, on a moonless night like tonight, when my cousins dared me to spend the night in the old balete tree. They were older and bigger and guided me into the big central hollow before sunset. And then I was alone, with just an old oil lamp and a bolo knife, in case there should be pythons about."

Carlos, who hated snakes, had eyes big as saucers.

"At first, I was so terrified I was sure I wouldn't sleep a wink! But I must've dozed off for when I woke my lamp had gone out. I hunted my pockets for matches, only to realize the lamp's dousing hadn't left me in darkness. I could see a luminous white glow filtering down through the twisted balete branches, and reflected on the oil lamp's glass chimney. Only, remember, it was a moonless night. It was not Mayari's kind eye peering down upon me, and truth be told, I almost looked up," Grandpa told us gravely.

"What was the glow?" I whispered.

"Maybe a Kapre's cigar, or a white lady's veil, a Santelmo or maybe..." Carlos whispered eagerly, more familiar with Grandpa's stories of the Philippines.

"Maybe," Grandpa agreed, "or maybe one of the anito, but I didn't look. You must never stare at an anito; most importantly, you must never stare into its eyes."

This seemed very reasonable to me, I hated staring into anyone's eyes.

"Why?" Nikki asked.

Grandpa regarded us solemnly, shadow falling rhythmically across his balding head with the slow circling of the lanai fans. "How old is Maya?"

"I'm almost nine!" I protested despite barely being eight.

Grandpa's expression changed, lightened, as if someone had yanked aside a curtain into a dimly lit room. "It's very rude to stare is all. And one must never be rude, particularly if you don't know who you're dealing with. What do we say to be respectful?"

"Tabi tabi po," we whispered, though this was clearly not the full story.

Grandpa checked his pocket watch. "I've kept you past Maya's bedtime. If Grandma hears she'll have my hide."

"But what did you do next? You have to tell us!" I begged.

"I grabbed my bolo, the same one I use today, though I've had to put a new pommel on it three times, and scrambled out of the balete fast as I could, praying to anyone who would listen that I wouldn't be followed home. And that's why I won't be hearing of you three messing around in the garden after dark. It's a miracle I didn't trip and break my neck." The eerie story was cut unceremoniously short, and we were waved off to bed.

"Maya's old enough for ghost stories," Carlos complained as we trooped away toward our shared bedroom that connected to the lanai.

"It won't be you she thrashes and kicks in the gut when she has nightmares, will it?" Nikki contended.

Carlos rolled his eyes.

"I'm not scared," I lied as a breeze blew from the garden into the screened lanai carrying the chime of dog tags and the sweet-spicy scent of plumeria.

Aside from "tabi tabi po" and strange dreams of glimmering swamp lights in the upper branches of the balete, our summer routine returned to normal. Though through my dreams I chased the glowing white form of Sampson deep into the garden till it was no longer the familiar spiral path and I was stumbling over twisting, twining balete roots, and the form up ahead didn't look very dog-shaped anymore. It almost looked like another kid, not much bigger than me.

Grandpa's voice echoed through my dreams, "Never be rude, and don't meet their eyes."

I kept my eyes on my sandy bare toes, and whispered, "Tabi tabi po."

At least I thought they were dreams. Nikki complained I was tracking sandy grey soil into the sheets, though I always wiped my feet carefully before climbing into the bed we shared.

I told Carlos my dreams.

"You two are just scaring each other. It's Florida, there's going to be sand everywhere," he said with a snort.

So the summer went on.

Mornings we walked to the beach to harass mole crabs, collect shells, and frolic in the surf. Then we'd hose off the sand and run wild in the backyard, playing blind man's bluff and catching anoles, staying close enough to the house so we'd hear Grandma calling us for lunch.

Every day Grandma tended her balete, only now instead of worm bin soil, she buried chicken bones and kitchen peelings around the base. And instead of old Sampson at her feet, Cosmo lounged in a comfortable hollow of the balete's trunk, six feet up, avoiding a hyper terrier mutt Grandpa had named Milo.

I never wondered at how fast the balete grew, swallowing up its palm host bit by bit, till I could see the balete's crown rising above the rest of the garden with the spreading palm fronds just out of its grasping reach. It wasn't just Grandma leaving offerings. I watched Cosmo drag roadkill into the balete and offer up decapitated bird heads in exchange for the choicest bits of chicken skin Grandma had buried that day.

Some nights I would sit out on the lanai, reading a book, watching the stars or maybe Grandpa's mysterious glowing visitor flicker among the upper branches in my peripheral vision. I told myself it was just the flash of Cosmo's eyes on his nighttime rambles, the sound of a child's voice in the garden, a trick of the wind. Still, its massive size was hardly a surprise. Everything Grandma touched grew. She said it was just the tropics and the Miracle Grow.

Her personal transplanted paradise.

What had originally been a barren plot of scraggly grass with three tall coconut palms was now a densely planted jungle, spreading mango trees and papaya leaves dancing in the salt breeze of incoming afternoon rains. Oleander, jasmine, and gumamela bloomed showy and bright among a thorny hedge of varied citrus trees. Hanging baskets of orchids lined the lanai. The garden always sprawled endlessly once my bare feet left the gritty textured tile of the lanai and lost myself within. My cousins and I grew up running wild through my grandmother's jungle, on green young coconuts, the flesh soft and chewy, the water within slightly rusty with the cut of my grandfather's bolo. They tended that garden like it was another one of us children, like a temple.

All summer I dreamed of chasing the flickering white flash of Sampson's fluffy tail through the garden undergrowth, past strange mutated citrus, with mottled hues and odd shapes, for which there was no name. Sometimes I didn't chase him alone, another child's hand tight in mine as we ran.

Though that wasn't a dream, I think. I don't know if some seeds don't breed true or if it was cross pollination, but the citrus grew strange, not at all how Grandma expected. They were kind of like us cousins that way, transplanted and growing different on foreign soil. But there remained something of the islands and Manila's golden sun still in the way we stood and the way our roots gripped the soil and our skin drank in light. We turned dark as coconut husks to Grandma's chagrin.

Or so Grandma told Grandpa one night out on the lanai when they thought we were asleep and Grandma's sleeping pills weren't working.

———◆———

The next morning, we tore into an orange as big as our heads, mottled green with yellow, with centers like bleeding hearts, so tart it made my tongue raw. Grandma made key lime pie from what was left, and offered us tiny calamansi that should have been tart but were pale green and sugar-sweet once you spat out all the seeds.

I watched Grandma fish seeds off our plates to sprout. Eventually, they'd graduate to pots on the lanai. Then finally Grandpa would dig a hole, six feet deep. We'd fill it almost to the top with layers of rich dark soil from the worm bins, lime, and fish bones, before planting the little citrus tree on top of the mound.

"Lots of oranges this year," Grandpa observed as he fed more into the juicer.

"They aren't quite oranges though," Carlos said.

Grandma hushed him. "Even an unexpected bounty is a blessing. We should give thanks for it." She led us in a second round of morning prayer before she whistled to Milo and went out to tend the garden. I always wondered but never asked why

Grandpa wasn't worried about Grandma spending so much time under the balete.

⸻ ◈ ⸻

The summer I was twelve and returned to Grandma's house, the balete tree had fully swallowed up its coconut palm host to peer over its vast domain.

Citrus season was ending, but the mangoes had just started to ripen. That summer our cousin trio fissured.

I suppose it was inevitable my older boy cousins would become embarrassed of me, their persistent tag-along. That summer they started spending hours closed inside a dimly lit arcade with friends. I tried to join them at first, convinced they'd grow tired of the place soon and we could go to the beach, but the cacophony of conflicting sounds, flashing lights, and the scent of hot plastic and teen boy proved too much of a deterrent.

I could only mope about with adults being helpful for so long. Luckily, I didn't roam the garden alone for long. I soon made a new friend who had no interest in being closed inside a dark arcade or vanishing to friends' houses to play computer games when there was a garden to explore, sandcastles to build and lizards to catch to populate my sand castle moats with monsters.

If Grandma thought me the wild child of our cousin gang, she had her hands full with my newest friend. I don't quite recall if they were a neighbor's kid or one of the kids of Grandma's old nursing colleagues she sometimes watched as a favor. But unlike most of the neighborhood kids, they never tired of my strange games or got lost in Grandma's garden.

We would tumble into the lanai, sticky from the heat and covered in dirt and Grandma would order us to the half-bath to wash up. She'd set the table with bowls overflowing with cut fruit. Huge green pulpy wedges of mystery citrus that would have put pomelo to shame, peeled like grapefruit from its tough interior skin, bright yellow slivers of mango like lost sunbeams. Rolls of suman, sticky and steaming, sat in their banana leaves, glistening pearl white on emerald like Grandma's favorite ear-rings. We weren't allowed to tear into the food like the pair of hungry raccoons that Grandpa chased away from his papaya trees at night, till we'd joined hands around the table and Grandma said grace with another murmured, "Tabi tabi po."

I echoed her like the phrase was indelibly linked to Amen.

I couldn't tell you what my new friend looked like. Mother reminds me I'm face blind and can't remember names to save my life. It usually didn't bother me I kept track of anyone who wasn't family by odd details. Like the neighbor with the curly blonde beard, and the church lady with the violet perfume who pinched my cheeks.

Still, I wish I could tell you my old friend's name. So much has faded, sun-bleached from my memory. Let us call them B. B had skin rough as bark with eczema that no amount of Grandma's coconut oil seemed to fix. They were dark and skinny as I was after a summer in the sun. They had a long tangling head of black hair that Grandma never wrestled into braids and buns like she did mine. They didn't visit all the time, but would find me when I was alone in the garden.

When I try to imagine their face now, all I can see is a blank bright whiteness, like the full moon on a cloudy evening and chasing Sampson's ghost through my dreams. But I liked how they held my hand in theirs, and the softness of their voice like the rustle of leaves.

Grandma liked my friend, though she told me, "You are not to follow them home, you don't want to impose."

Grandma reminded me often, especially on days B visited, never to walk to the balete if she wasn't with us.

I only disobeyed her once.

Tabi tabi po.

My cousins had gotten invited to an overnight LAN party and I found sleeping alone in our shared room impossible. I snuck out onto the lanai with my book, but my reading light batteries were failing. That's when I saw B, lingering at the entrance to the spiral garden path, nervous as a cat to be caught.

After a quick check that my grandparents' lights were out, I passed through the kitchen for snacks. I left Milo a handful of corn pops to buy his silence and snuck into the garden to join B.

I don't remember suggesting the caper, but B told me that Cosmo had taken something of theirs up into his hang-out hollow in the balete. We had to stack Grandma's gardening chair on top of the old bonsai table, but with much giggling and barefooted scrambling, we clambered up.

It was roomier than I'd expected and Cosmo had quite a nest for himself, lined with stolen socks, hair ties, and several tv remotes. Grandma had been blaming Grandpa for misplacing them. After tossing down the remotes, I helped B tie on the red thread and coral bracelet Grandma had given them. Then, having achieved our objective and a lofty perch, we settled into the comfy hollow sharing handfuls of corn pops straight out of the bag, reveling at this secret adventure, and jumping and clutching at each other at every night sound filtering to us from the garden.

Suddenly, a crashing noise out in the garden that was *not* raccoon-sized started near the outer edge of the spiral path. Terrified gooseflesh spread over my arms. I wasn't sure if I was more afraid Grandma would find me out in the garden at night or we'd get eaten by whatever lived in the balete for trespassing.

Tabi tabi po.

It sounded like a herd of elephants were trying to force their way through the garden's dense plantings. B leaned down from our perch and knocked aside Grandma's gardening chair concealing our ascent. I pulled my legs up, and scuttled into the depths of the hollow, pressing tight against B's side. Whatever was coming wasn't coming from the balete. Though somehow there was significantly more space in the depths of our perch than there had been. I was glad we could pull back, out of sight.

Yellow beams of flashlights shone erratically through the leaves and a pack of unfamiliar older teens burst into the center of the garden, crushing border plantings and breaking branches. They were much bigger than my twelve-and-a-half.

"What are these? They look diseased!" One boy stepped around the dense hedges knocking citrus fruits down and smashing the ripe fruit under his feet.

The sharp scent of zest mixed with sweet-sticky fruit innards. I heard the shattering of glass and the sharp scent of alcohol reached our perch.

"Watch it!"

"It was already empty."

"I hear the old man walks around with a knife as tall as he is."

"I bet he uses it to skin trespassers alive!"

"I heard the old hag is a voodoo witch."

Then someone pulled open a backpack and started distributing toilet paper rolls. B shook like a leaf beside me, their chin hooked into my shoulder, their bony arms locked tight around me.

I watched the first roll fly up, past our hiding place, white streaming behind it and catching moonbeams. Then the screaming started.

The whole balete shook, like a palm in hurricane winds. I clung desperately to the rough bark, trying not to be shaken from our hiding place. The shaking made the roots look like they were lashing like a frightened octopus, or maybe that was just B, who was latched around me tight, half clambered around my waist.

When I tried to lean forward to see what was happening, their tangled hair fell over my eyes. I only saw a frightened white face disappearing under the balete's tangled roots.

B squeezed tighter and tighter. I could hardly breathe, the balete shuddered, the hollow seeming to press around us like a swallowing throat, so tight I feared we'd be crushed. I must have passed out due to lack of air and sheer terror.

—⟨◈⟩—

In the morning broken glass glittered like dew on the garden stones. Grandpa swept the glass into trash bags with the broken limbs and smashed fruit. Then he carried out the ladder he used to harvest papaya and lifted B and I down from the balete.

Cosmo yowled and climbed up to take our place, upset his nest had been disturbed.

There was no sign of the toilet paper, the backpack, or the boys.

"Nako, don't tell your grandma." Grandpa made us swear. "And tell me what you stole so I can replace it before she notices. Aren't you two a bit young to be breaking into my alcohol cabinet? I'd expect that kind of nonsense from Carlos, not you."

He frowned at the broken tree limbs and smashed fruit around the center of the garden. "We'll tell Grandma the raccoons got into fermented fruit."

B and I nodded our agreement with this cover story wildly. I surreptitiously kicked sand over a scrap of red fabric caught among the balete's roots.

Grandpa peered down at us. "You're sure you don't feel sick? How did you get up that high?"

"Put the chair on the table," I admitted.

Grandpa frowned at the glass glittering in his trash bag. "I don't even remember buying flavored vodka...must've been your grandma for her ladies nights."

"Sorry! I was looking for a snack and it smelled sweet. I thought it was soda." I spun my tale wildly. Overhead, a roll of toilet paper was wedged in the crown of the balete. A short length of white paper fluttered in the breeze. I squeezed B's hand tight. They squeezed back.

Hurricane Gordon made landfall in the winter two years later.

When Grandma and Grandpa refused to evacuate, Mom pulled me out of school at midday, tossed me in the back of the car and drove south to get them herself. She practically dragged them away from battening down the garden. We spent three days without power, my cousins and I camping on the floor of the living room, the house full to bursting with family.

The eye of the storm was miles off but it rained and rained for a week. Even Grandma's sleeping pills couldn't keep up with her pacing. Some nights I would sit at the end of the hall with a book while she paced up and down, up and down.

When I asked Grandma if my friend B had evacuated, she burst into tears.

When it was finally safe for everyone to go home, I insisted on going along to see how the garden had fared.

The drive down was terrible. Roofs were blown away and orchards ravaged. Ripe oranges scattered between the rows, beside trees torn out by the roots. Mom was forced to re-route three times to avoid flooded crossings, fallen trees, and downed powerlines.

The closer we got to their house, the quieter and paler Grandma became. Grandpa reached forward from the back seat beside me to grip her hand. I braced for the worst when we turned onto their street at last. Shattered roofing tiles littered the road. Glass glittered on lawns like frost in the sunshine.

Drifts of oleander flowers from Grandma's bushes lined the driveway like funereal offerings. While the adults circled the house to inspect the roof and windows I hurried toward the garden, my feet slip-sliding in muddy standing water till I tripped, skinning my hands on the first paving stone of the spiral path. Blood welled up on my palms dripping onto the muddy petal-strewn ground. I looked back and realized I hadn't tripped over a fallen roofing tile or downed branch, but one of the gnarled roots of the balete that reached the edges of the yard. I stared up at the spreading branches of the balete huddled over the garden like a mother hen over chicks.

Wiping my smarting hands on my shirt I whispered, "Tabi tabi po," and began walking the spiral to the center. Not a branch had snapped nor a single leaf had fallen, but every blooming flower had been plucked from its bush. Finally I reached the center, where the trunk of the balete was heaped in fallen petals like drifts of strange snow, an offering to its protection. The air smelled so spiced with perfume I almost didn't notice the sweet hint of decay.

My head spun. Under the drifts of flowers there were bodies. I wondered how much the balete had eaten that there were leftovers. A big silvery tarpon with its shovel-shaped snout had swum through flood waters far from the canal and gotten trapped among the balete's tangling roots. I saw matted tufts of fur of a fat palm rat, I gulped and minced forward, wondering if I might see more humanoid shapes...after all, our balete must've been very hungry without Grandma's offerings of chicken bones and table scraps.

Someone took my stinging hand in theirs, squeezing tight, as they pulled me from the sight. Only it wasn't Grandma, or Grandpa, or Mom. It was B. Their grip was small and rough and strong. I turned into them, hugging them tight. I was so glad they'd come through the storm safe, I thought my heart would burst.

I didn't ask them how their house had fared in the storm, though I should have. I only led them inside where the adults were pulling together a meal of canned goods from the pantry, while Grandpa gathered all the rotting food from the fridge to put into the worm bins. B and I didn't say a word about the balete, just like we'd never said a word about that night after Grandma bought a raccoon trap to keep the rascals out of her garden. Instead, I showed B the latest books I was reading on the lanai, staying out from under the adults' feet.

Despite our secrecy and my grandparents' effusive relief that their home was undamaged, my mother grew more upset all evening, her gaze skimming over us kids, B and I, in short flickering glances, her lips pressed tight together.

"Maya, come help me with—"

Grandpa cut her off, "Let them play, they are perfectly safe now the storm's past."

They switched into hurried Tagalog. I caught my mother's concern about storms and tree branches, but none had fallen so I disregarded her worries, pressing close to B's side and trying to ignore the scent of rotten flesh and bruised flowers following us in from the garden.

Grandma cooked spam and kimchi fried rice over the little butane stove she used on the lanai when she cooked daing, salted dried sardines, that we cousins affectionately referred to as "stinky fish". Grandma offered B a few bites of crispy spam while the rest of the food cooked, insisting they were underfed, and needed more meat on their bones.

When the food was ready, Grandma said a long and heart-felt grace that their home and the garden had no major damage, tag-ending Amen with tabi tabi po, which my mother, unused to this ritual, echoed late, frown lines ever deepening.

We ate off paper plates, huddled on the lanai to catch the last of the sun. There was still no power. B was hungry and ate three servings before vanishing back into the garden to head home. I remember my mother staring at me all through dinner like I'd grown two heads, though I must've told her about B before.

I'm not sure if it was my mom meeting B or her new job, but that was the last summer she sent me to stay at Grandma's with my cousins.

When Grandma complained of the lack of visits, Mom said her new job paid more so she didn't need her summer traveling nursing contract jobs to make extra money. But we still didn't visit till Grandpa intervened and Mom and Grandma had a heart to heart. Finally, we began to visit more often, but just for a week, and something about Mom's watchful eye meant we cousins never really got into the kinds of shenanigans we usually did, though maybe that was just growing older. By then Carlos was entering high school and B hardly ever came around, and never when Mom was with me.

I missed B and the easy wordless communication of our garden games, the squeeze of their hand in mine.

The last time I saw them was years later, a few months after Grandpa's funeral. Mom was busy with work. Carlos and Nikki were at college in the middle of finals. I'd driven down from Tallahassee on my own.

I spent all week helping Grandma tidy the garden. Without Grandpa to help her, things had gone wild. It took me three days to clear the path to the old balete tree. The spirals were more a maze with thorny screens of key lime and calamansi as tall as I was and several feet thick with thorns the length of my little finger. B showed up to help, bagging cut limbs and raking up debris along my hacked path so Grandma wouldn't try to bend over to help. They confided that Grandma was sad when she couldn't walk her prayer path.

Grandpa's gardening bolo fit well in my hand and made quick work of even the most stubborn tree limbs. Once the path was clear, Grandma prepared a feast of fluffy white rice, vinegar stewed adobo, all unsalted, and cut fruit served up on a platter lined with guava leaves that she had me carry to the balete and lay among its roots.

Grandma's prayers sounded like an apology for being away so long. On the way back, she walked me through all the pruning, fertilizing, and harvesting schedules for her most treasured plants. I took good notes. She showed me where she'd cordoned off the children of the mutant citrus that had grown the summer the balete escaped its pot. Through a thicket too dense for me to brave even with the protection of Grandpa's bolo, I peered into a world of feral citrus in all stages of growth. Some trees bloomed white and pink, yellow pollen drifting through the air. Some hung heavy with fruit, all grown large on the decomposing lumps of citrus already fallen, filling the air with the toothache-sweet scent of decay. I couldn't manage it, but B waded in without fear, impervious to thorns, and emerged without a scratch on them. We tore into the strange fruits with relish. Juice dripped down our chins.

It was like childhood returned, caught in the thorny branches overhead. I leaned into their bony shoulder and rested my head against their neck.

"Sorry I've been gone so long," I said, "I never meant to, but time got away from me."

I'd figured out some things about myself since those spindly gawkish years from twelve to fifteen, that explained a lot about why Mom hadn't wanted me spending summers at Grandma's anymore. I'd cut my frizzy frustrating hair into a pixie cut that barely touched my ears. I'd kissed a cheerleader behind the bleachers at senior homecoming, even though she attended the dance with a pimple-faced footballer who'd asked her. She'd been too embarrassed to say no after he wrote her name on placards in the crowd.

B rested their still sticky cheek on the top of my head, "I'm glad you came back. Will you stay this time?"

"I think so, Grandma needs someone. She shouldn't be alone."

B nodded and we carried the biggest and sweetest fruits inside to Grandma.

All week, I'd come in from the garden, sweat-stained and sticky, and wash up in the half-bath before heading in to where Grandma was scrubbing the latest fruits of my labor: mango so ripe it was nearly fermented and papaya longer than my arms, and of course her beloved mutant citrus which made her happiest of all.

"It's far too hot to cook," Grandma said, after her initial foray into the kitchen to sate the balete's hunger. We feasted on fruit and drank cold ginger tea, and everything tasted of childhood summers.

I caught myself sneaking a bite of papaya under the table, only there was no wet nose bumping my hand for tidbits. "Should I go to the pound tomorrow? I could find an older cat or dog to keep you company, something low maintenance."

I'd been outside most of the time, but the house was so quiet without Grandpa or little Milo or Grandpa's cat, Cosmo, who'd climbed up to his favorite perch in the balete tree and gone to sleep one last time, a week after Grandpa died.

Grandma patted my hand. "The house and garden keep me more than busy." She smiled sadly. "It's too much if I'm honest; I'm a little too old."

I squeezed her hand tightly and we watched the sun set red and gold into the deep green of the garden in silence, before I collected our dishes to rinse them before the fruit juice attracted ants.

"Have you started thinking about schools?" she asked.

"Carlos and Nikki think I should go out of state like them." I winked at her over my shoulder.

Her sour expression was priceless.

"Nonsense. Too wild, the two of them by half. I saw a picture of Nikki NAKED! Naked, on the front page of his school newspaper. Walang hiya! Gallivanting about for the whole world to see!"

"Mom thinks I should stay local. Attend community college in Tallahassee first."

Grandma's nose wrinkled. "No, you are too clever. If you go to UF, you will be only twenty minutes from here. You could stay at the house, it's cheaper than the dorms."

"UF is my first choice, in state."

"Think of how much money you'll save compared to out of state," Grandma wheedled.

I agreed. Grandma needed someone here with her more than my mom needed me to stay underfoot.

"You remember, the house will be here for you, and if you could see to the garden it would make me very happy."

I stayed up that night, reading on the lanai, enjoying the salty ocean breeze. Grandma puttered about, which caught us in a contest of who'd give in first, but Grandma was more experienced with sleeplessness. I was soon yawning, the words swimming on the page.

Grandma brought me a cup of tea. "You ought to turn in now."

"What about you?" I asked.

"Oh, old people don't need much sleep. Besides, my sleeping pills haven't been working very well since Grandpa...is the garden path clear now? I might walk my prayer spiral. That always settles me."

"Would you like me to walk with you?" I asked, a bit worried she might trip in the dark.

"No, no, I'll be a while and you look so tired."

I protested, but a jaw-cracking yawn caught me mid-sentence and so I gave in, clutching the warm cup of ginger tea and settling deeper into the cushioned chair.

The moon was full, and now that I wasn't trying to focus on the page, the night was practically bright. Grandma would be fine. She knew her garden better than anyone, except maybe B.

I watched sleepily as Grandma toed off her velvet house slippers for garden shoes and set off slowly down the path. Her opening Ave Maria drifted to me on the breeze. The outer rings of the garden were thin enough that I could watch her make the first three circuits.

I blinked and must've slept, or dreamed. I was small again, chasing the flickering white glow of Sampson's tail through the garden. Only in this dream I sat on a rocking chair in the lanai, watching the white glow of something no longer dog-shaped meander along the prayer path beside Grandma. Grandpa's lessons were well-learned and I did not stare, only watching the flicker of shadows and silhouette in my periphery, as I watched the moon set into the dense leafy green.

The moonlight played tricks with time, twirling it around lazy fingers like strands of Spanish moss, till the balete tree was small, and I was a child again, only sneaking out to the porch to read where my penlight would not disturb my cousins. I could hear their sleeping breaths and muttering just over the familiar thrum of the lanai fan. I might wander across the house to find Grandma sleeping peacefully while Grandpa read by the light of their bedside lamp, with old Cosmo purring in his lap.

When I woke, with a start, to a splatter of a cold morning rain, my teacup rolled off my lap and shattered on the tile of the lanai.

I didn't think to look for Grandma till after I'd cleaned up the mess and bandaged my bleeding foot.

By the time I found her, chin on her chest, hands folded peacefully in her lap, on her gardening chair quite sheltered and protected under the balete tree, she'd gone as cold and stiff as dear old Sampson.

The wind blew through the garden carrying the scent of plumeria and the chiming of dog tags.

B's hand slid into mine, giving a comforting squeeze.

Tabi tabi po.

Star Crossed

Valo Wing

Content Warnings: Mentions of suicide

Dying, of course, had always been our plan.

But now, with Ro sprawled in shadows on the other side of our candlelight-splashed tomb, brows devastatingly furrowed as they scribble the details of yet another failed attempt in a worn journal, I wonder—and not for the first time—if we severely miscalculated.

Because we can't seem to stop.

One vertebra at a time, I peel off the icy stone floor. The fresh stab wound in my chest screams. Sinew and bone, muscle and skin, tangle its fingers together, going about the business of making me appear whole. I wriggle my toes within their prison of satin slippers. Bring bloodied fingers to tear the fabric of my dress from its low neckline to waist. Slip free. Exhale relief.

Ro glances from the journal to me, mischievous gaze traveling north to south, then north again. "Every time, Liet." They laugh. "Don't get me wrong, I enjoy the show—" A twitch at the corner of their mouth. "But you're so lovely in that gown."

"Yeah, well, it's not for your enjoyment," I snipe.

Ro's mouth parts, mock-wounded, pen dripping ink between long, pale fingers.

"Fine, maybe a little," I begrudge, hating myself. "I just … can't take it anymore. Each death returning me to this damn outfit, this cursed"—I rip at the long strands of burnished gold magically regrown and tumbling to my waist—"*hair*. For once, I'd love it if dying and resurrecting didn't mean…" I can't finish the sentence. Wraiths welcome me home. The tomb is cold.

Silence stretches agonizingly between us.

Then, Ro, sotto voce and dry: "You always cut your hair and dress as you like when we're"—they gesture vaguely—"*out there*."

Black lightning crackles in my veins. "And that's supposed to be enough? At least you knew who you were half a millennium ago. Had family support. I wasn't granted such freedom." Pain, nebula explosion; violent in my veins. "My apologies for being unable to accept a few stolen hours here and there, knowing no matter what I do, I always wind up looking as I did that damn night."

"Hey, now! That's our wedding night you're damning."

"Technically," I correct, stepping out of burgundy satin (sweet relief!), "the night after."

"Semantics."

"You're being an asshole."

Ro runs a hand through their short, curly hair. Grins. A dark strand falls over one eye. "Shall I make it up to you, then? Come *here*, darling. Please. I'm wretched and starving for you. My fingers tremble for your skin, my bones ache. Soothe my need, appease my thirst."

"A *dramatic* asshole," I amend.

The hole in my chest finishes suturing itself. I exhale and the pain becomes a ghost, joining the myriad other specters haunting this crypt. Shadowy fingers press bruises in my sides, leave reminders of each story, each end, we've sung. My body, nothing more than a canvas of memories, cells never regenerating, never shedding to become new.

Ro flips the pen between their fingers. Muses, "I do love it when we wake in New York. Thought our last performance went pretty well, too. The Met is my favorite stage to die on."

"It's dusty and the curtains smell of sweat," I complain.

"But the chandeliers! When they rise to the ceiling it's like watching a meteoroid shower in reverse."

"Big disagree." Those chandeliers could never come close to the real thing.

Ro's mouth thins. "Okay, you're being terribly cross this resurrection."

"Yeah? Bite me."

They snort, expression wicked. "Come closer and I will."

Stubborn, I kick away the fabric puddle gathered about my feet. Walk to the nearest wall in nothing but my now anachronistic undergarments, encircling the length of our prison, dragging two fingers along cold stone. Candles gutter in my wake. Ghosts cling to my shoulder blades. I stop once I've circled the entire perimeter; stand above Ro like a desperate, invisible god.

They tip back their head, shut their eyes. "You have to admit the productions are infinitely better than they were a hundred-something years ago; that last one wasn't even trying to be subtle about my role not being a man—for the first time, it actually *felt* like us up there." They hum a snippet of Bellini's final duet.

I stare into the emptiness of our crypt, an icy dark bereft of stars. "Speak for yourself."

A sigh. "Come *here*, beautiful." They reach for me and I relent.

Sliding onto their lap, I plunge my nose into the warmth of their neck. Inhale poison and sweat and blood. Home. One of their hands comes about my waist. Despite it all, we still have each other. Solidarity in this strange hell. We've never been separated. And I love them, even now. Even though I am changed and so much more while they remain the same.

Pulling me close, they slide their second hand around me, tangling in strands of my long hair. A small growl escapes their lips. They love me like this. And although it brings me pain, I can suffer these small moments so long as they welcome the real me *out there*.

Which I know they do.

The journal slips from their fingers and falls open on the dark floor. I move to push it away.

And stare in disbelief.

In the beginning, we used to huddle together, them recording every aspect of our latest venture, me watching over their shoulder, looking for any clue, any key to break us from this endless cycle of death and rebirth. But the years stretch on, and I've left them to it. For our fate has yet to alter, despite our location and circumstance and year. Always the same, every time. Where they go, I follow. Two meandering shadows glued to one another, fated never to part, tasting only a glimpse of life before—

Poison. And a knife.

And I can no longer stomach reliving our demise on paper knowing we'll reenact it in person all too soon. Ro assured me they could handle the task and has dutifully continued the records upon each return to the tomb.

Except.

I see no writing on the page. Instead, sketches cover every inch of white: the stages we've sung on, the food we've eaten, city skylines, those fleeting encounters with people who have no idea who we are and no idea we'll never cross paths again. And, also, images of me. Except ... not. Sketches of Liet through their eyes; the Liet of their dreams. Liet of their youth. Liet of whispered wedding vows. Someone false. Someone not real.

Liet of the tomb.

"What is this?" I hiss, swiping the journal from the floor.

They scrabble uselessly at the backs of my hands, but I have the journal and I'm not letting go. I jump from their lap. Stumble to the far wall. Bile burns in my throat, the pressing dark too severe, no longer safe and welcome. Page after page, the same. I swallow lightning and broken glass. Another turn of the page. All alike. Clearly, they stopped analyzing our journeys, stopped looking for the crack into which we could wriggle free some time ago. Fine. That, I can accept. But this, these sketches of me always in that vile gown, my hair long and plaited and crowned in roses, this I cannot stand.

"Give it back, Liet." Their voice, quiet but unmoving.

"All these years." I will not break for them to watch; my body now more iron, more steel than flesh and blood. "All these years, and this is *still* how you see me? When you know it's not true, when you know how unhappy, how trapped I feel here in the tomb and on the stage? This is the spouse you want?"

They spread their hands, palms up. Say, simply: "You're beautiful."

"But only like this."

Ro bites their lower lip. Refuses to look at me.

"You don't want us to break free," I accuse. The journal escapes my fingers and thuds dully on the floor. "You love this purgatory we're in."

It was only supposed to be once; one dramatic performance, one extravagant lie, in exchange for a lifetime of freedom. Instead, we keep dying. Doomed to play our roles ad nauseam with no sign of relief.

Still, without meeting my gaze: "I thought you'd have realized that by now."

Oily shadows smooth vicious valleys in Ro's face beneath bladed cheekbones. I wonder—a touch daftly—if the next time we find ourselves on stage, I could simply pluck the bones from their face; stab myself with them instead of whatever knife I'm handed by the stage crew. Slide the diamond edge between my ribs, soft as a sigh.

Poison wafts from their skin, heavy in the velvet darkness, bruisingly saccharine, and I can't do this; I need stars, I need the darkness of real night.

I stagger. They're across the crypt in a comet-flash, one arm around my waist. "Don't," I plead. "Please." I can no longer stand the chivalry when they won't accept it in return, I can't—

"Hush, darling." Their lips a brush against my ear. "It's going to be alright."

"It's not." I blink rage-water from my eyes, take in the familiar crypt, effervescently dark, blistering black and velvet; home. "This is no life."

Their grip on me tightens, lips insistent against skin. "And who's to dictate what makes a life? It may not be conventional, but it's *ours*."

"Things are different now, Ro. I see them, in the audience, past the fourth wall, phantomlike and blurred, only there and real. People like us—lovers, who don't have to hide." My nails curl into their wrist, desperate. "We're finally in an age where being ourselves might be safe, if we could just find a way to break the cycle—"

"And? Spend a handful of years together, then die? What we have is a gift. What we have is forever."

Forever.

"You're wrong." My voice, brittle-sharp: "This is no gift."

Ro nips at my ear and withdraws, clearly exasperated. "Such a pessimist, lover."

Darkness swirls about their ankles as they walk to the other side of the tomb, swipe the journal from where I dropped it. They slide down the wall and flip through the pages. I battle nauseous jealousy at the easy set to their shoulders, the vest unbuttoned and collared shirt beneath, wrinkled yet true.

Ro—who faked their death as a child to live the life they wanted, whose family supported the decision and told the world they'd adopted a son to try and appease their grief over the loss of their daughter—never has to suffer as I do. When we fell in love and the secret came out, they told me we could do it again; feign death to achieve freedom. Blitzed by youthful infatuation, I agreed. Little did I know, each return to this tomb they'd remain themself, while my noose tightened. I thought at least they understood my rage, my despair, my grief.

But the journal proves they see only the person they wish I was. And I don't know how to change that. Or if it's even possible for someone like them to like the real me. And yet …

At the end of our most recent second act, two women(?) sat in the front row, hand in hand. They carried themselves similarly, both in trousers, both with short hair. A confident gleam in two sets of eyes. As Ro drank the poison, leaving me to fall upon them—inconsolable and tragic, blade in my ribs, blood spilling forth—I focused on the two faces in the front row until the curtain came down, dragging me home. On the way they looked at each other with blatant and unquenchable desire. The way they rose to their feet amidst the applause (our requiem) proud and sure. When the opera ended, they would walk back to their lives, untethered and free.

To have what they do with Ro …

It's possible. It has to be.

A glitter of gold in the shadows. Ozone in the air. The tomb tilts; a world jolted from its axis. Vertigo sings within my chest. Two beings unfolded. A blink, an exhale, and—

"New York?" Ro shoves up on their elbows in the middle of Central Park. Above; a sky of blue and wispy white tinged gray with smog. "But we were just here."

And so it begins again.

"Thought you loved New York," I grumble, avoiding the pointed stares from passing people who clearly think we're actors on break from some Shakespearean production. I'm not sure what returned us already to Manhattan; our resurrections normally randomized; wherever in the world, through whichever media form happens to be showcasing our tragedy at the time.

Warmed summer grass and asphalt collide in my nose. I sit, brushing freshly cut blades from my ancient undergarments. In my veins, the shimmer of anticipation, despite the bitter knowledge of how the charade plays out. At least I get a few precious hours first. And I treasure them. Possibly more than anything. Maybe even more than Ro. "Come on. I need new clothes. And a haircut."

They groan, pushing me to my back. The sky becomes their face; laughing and handsome and eternally young. "Can't you keep it long? Just this once? For me?" They brush a kiss on my forehead, my temple, the corner of my mouth. "You're so beautiful, my Liet, my love, my—"

I remember the journal; the sketches. The fact that no matter how many times we resurrect, how many times I chop my hair and buy new clothes, I always return the Liet I was when we met. My heart roars.

The years crash about me. The pain and the blood and the music and the lights and the applause. The betrayal and lies. The end. For that's all Ro and I will ever be: a constant end, on loop until the planet melts in flames. Until the universe as we know it is no longer recognizable, changed indeterminately for both the better and worse. And although we were granted a beginning, mine was false, while they had the chance to start over. So, for us, a beginning and an end. Never a middle. Always, an end.

I shove them off. Scowl. "No."

They groan in encore, over-dramatic, then stand and hold forth an ink-stained hand for me to grasp. "As you wish, wife. Let's find you a barber before it's time to die."

To die and die and die.

I move to shove my hands in my pockets, but these clothes don't have any. Of course they don't. Fury crashes in my ears. Ro walks ahead of me, tall and shoulders straight. Hands out of sight, an infuriating whistle leaves their lips.

I ignore them until after my hair has been shorn off, the weight gone, new clothes acquired thanks to the money that magically appeared in their pocket.

When we exit the Fifth Avenue department store, gleaming windows many stories high reflect the me I know in secret and love. Pulse a vivid accelerando, I want to weep, to scream, to grab Ro around the waist and swing them about in wild joy. This particular barber did an excellent job, my gilded strands artfully tousled yet erect, the back of my neck exposed to the wind and sky. I adjust the lapels of my new sapphire suit. Smile wide and turn my head to examine the severity of my profile, the jut of strong nose and square jaw. Golden hour surrounds us, limning Ro with intoxicating light. They're devilishly striking, like a god. The supposed love of my never-ending existence. I move to kiss them, to pull them close in this sacred time before we must don our costumes and act out our inevitable demise.

They quirk an eyebrow and dodge me, quick. "We're going to be late."

Right. Can't have that.

Dejected, I shoulder past and make for Lincoln Center while New York howls and hisses with vibrant life.

The Met glitters pearly white and diamond-bright, smearing sunset in watercolor pastels over swarming couples eager for this night's performance. I halt at the central fountain, inhale water droplets and beg a silent prayer for things to be different.

"Liet," snaps Ro.

I lick my lips, taste imminent death, and murmur: "Meet you in there."

They sigh and leave my side without so much as a loving touch, a kiss, or glance. It shouldn't matter. It *doesn't* matter. In the end, it's always the same. I'll blink and be on stage, dressed in another wretched gown, scratchy wig dug into my skull, a fresh knife in my hands.

"Please tell me this opera pisses you off, too."

Surprised, I turn, taking in the person standing at the fountain beside me: hands thrust in the pockets of their white suit, brown skin luminous, short, dark hair wavy and caught in the breeze. No one ever speaks to us when we're here. Not unless we initiate. Ro and I; eternal wraiths, shadow-beings who slither along the recesses of reality. "Excuse me?"

They snort lightly, glance at me askance. "I always find myself wondering what would happen if she drank the poison first, leaving the knife for him."

A storm, previously unseen and unrealized, whispers through my veins, crescendos over the miracle of a stranger's unprompted voice directed at me. But ... drink the poison first? Impossible. "You've seen this production a lot, then?"

"This *story*," they correct, mouth twisting. "In pretty much every form it exists. Opera, ballet, play, movie. I despise them all but can't seem to quit—call me a masochist, I just"—they grimace and something takes flight in my chest—"keep waiting for someone to come along and tell it differently. Oh well. Hanging onto hope." They laugh and hold out a hand, rings on every finger. "Ignore me. I've heard this show's two stars are phenomenal. I'm sure it'll be great. I'll sit and watch in agony, then drink myself into oblivion to forget I keep putting myself through this. Imara, by the way. They/she."

Imara's hand is warm, the many rings cool against my skin.

"Liet," I offer. Then, swift as a thunderclap, and, without hesitation although never before verbalized to Ro or anyone else, "They/them."

"Nice to meet you, Liet." They smile, gaze lingering on my mouth, my nose, my hair, before coming to rest on my eyes. "Any chance I can sweep you off your feet for something a little more affirming? Care to ditch this bullshit?"

A breeze caresses my brow, loosening a strand of hair. I sweep it off my forehead. Clear my throat. "Ah, I'm uh, kind of expected in there."

"A date?" She smiles crooked, exposing the world's most perfect singular dimple.

"I suppose that's one word for it." The stage, the costumes, the conductor and lights. The knife. Ro and their plaintive wails before drinking the poison, leaving me to follow behind. Death. Then the tomb. Always, the tomb. My long hair returned, my bridal gown pristine, the fresh hole in my chest screaming shut. Ro and their journal, sketching the person they wished I was instead of the person I am.

Doubt crackles unsteady but electric sharp beneath my skin. A swirling storm of lightning and shadows glitter in my lungs.

Hunger. Desperation. "Actually, you know what? Why not. I know a place, if you're interested."

Imara smiles glorious as dawn. "Awesome!"

We fall into step, side by side. I don't look back at the opera house, at Ro waiting impatient within. Any moment we'll be reunited, any moment the earth will tilt and I'll be on the stage, lungs full of lies, throat full of false words, tongue sharpened and ready for blood.

But maybe, just this once, I can procrastinate.

Together we cross the street, towards Hotel Empire. I saw the invite on Ro's magically materialized phone earlier this afternoon; a glamorous cast party post-performance that we'd never be able to attend. Well, fuck that. My suit is exquisite; the stage hasn't summoned me yet. And, too, this stranger at my side; ravishing beyond belief. When I rush to the door and hold it open for them, a small smile tugs at the corner of her mouth. The elevator ride skyward is a quiet affair, the both of us sneaking glances and pretending we're not, hands somehow incapable of leaving our pockets. I lean into the wall, crossing one ankle in front of the other, counting every beat of my heart, every inhale that's *mine* and mine alone. Before fate calls me home.

Shiny doors glide open, revealing a modern penthouse. Greenery, flower arches, entire trees, decorate the interior. The air's perfumed by lilac and peony. Votive candles flicker a warmer yellow than the anemic glow of those in our tomb. Laughter and the clink of crystal glasses pull us deeper, the event still being set up, empty save for us and hired staff.

"What is this?" Imara asks, eyes wide and glittering.

I bite my lower lip in attempt to hold back the grin blossoming. My throat, molten gold. The powdered glass in my veins somehow softer. "Maybe a place we can tell our own story instead of sitting through someone else's."

A stranger greets me with confused enthusiasm at our early arrival. Leads us through the forest until we enter a room lined with racks of clothes. They gesture, saying, "Pick out whatever you like, it's part of this," then leave us alone.

No. Granite squeezes my heart; diamonds broken and dull scrape their knuckles over my wounded soul. I look to Imara. Say, resolute, "I'm not wearing a costume." The very word a poison to my ears.

"That's fair, me neith—" She whistles low through her teeth. "Wait, holy shit, I need this."

Apprehensive, I come to their side, watch as she shoves dresses and suits aside to reveal a spectacular set of faux chainmail and pauldrons. My tongue salivates with inexplicable want.

She glances at me and chuckles. "There's more than one. We can both wear armor if you'd like, no rules against it."

Unable to speak, I nod, reaching for silver. Slip out of my suit jacket and pull metal over my head. Imara helps strap the pauldrons over my shoulders, her touch soft, yet sure. I help her in turn. My pulse has sped, and I know any moment now I'll blink, be on that stage, staring into Ro's familiar self-assured face. But I can't go back, I can't suffer it anymore, I need—

"Shall we?" I extend my hand. They twist their fingers into mine.

We enter the main room, resplendent. Floor-to-ceiling windows expose Central Park, the sun almost vanished, sky nothing more than a violet smudge of atmosphere. I pray for stars. For those celestial orbs denied to me since the night of my wedding hundreds of years ago. Of late, all I know is day, and the dark of the stage. The dark of the tomb. And there are no stars in those places.

Imara guides me to the balcony. Outside, the air is cool, velvet-soft and full of promise. I hold my breath. Count the beats of my heart, every thrum closer to tearing me from this moment, this magic, this gift. We stand, side by side, hands gripping the silver railing. I catch her watching me, eyes sparkling, naked want trapped in the corners of her lips. Wings erupt from my veins, formed of glass shards previously designed to hurt, now magnificent and pearlescent.

"What?" I tease as their smile becomes something mischievous.

She shakes her head. Swipes a hand through short hair, faux armor gleaming quicksilver radiant. "I just"—they break off, eyeing me again—"can't believe I convinced someone *this* hot, a total stranger, too, to ditch their plans and be my date for the most absurd party of the year."

Brightness. Ringing in my heart. A roar to the wet fire of my blood. The catch of strange light on mirrored skyscrapers glimmering and dusted in shadows. Darkness blooms. I'm supposed to be on stage. I *should* be on the stage. Ro is most likely beside themself.

Courage, now.

I sink to one knee. Reach for her hand. They place it gentle and obliging in mine. I draw brown knuckles to my mouth. Press a lingering kiss to skin smelling of hope and stars and joy.

Raise my eyes to theirs, slowly, oh so slow, for I fear when I look up she'll be gone and I'll be returned to the tomb. Always the tomb. Always Ro and death and a game of pretend. Our plot, our desperate ploy for freedom twisting us in mocking fingers. We planned to die. But maybe, just maybe, I finally want to live. For this night, this armor, this exhale.

For me.

Darkness smiles. I look to the sky, searching for stars and instead find a night luminous and laughing lit by the myriad jeweled lights of the city. For a moment, Imara's hand in mine becomes the knife. Poised and ready, so used to my grip, my resignation. For a moment, I forget to breathe, convinced blades will erupt from knuckles and spear me through. Across the avenue, Ro hesitates, their usual cue gone, unsure what to do without me there. Confused as to why I'm not. Wondering what changed this time when it never has before.

Ro: unable to sing without me, unable to play their part, unable to fathom any other way.

Well. How very sad for them.

Calm and certain, I rise.

Imara winds her fingers around the back of my neck, thumb grazing my jaw, irises a beautiful dark. "Goddamn," she murmurs. "Who the hell even are you?"

Catching their chin in my hands, I lean close. Inhale and smell freedom. "Someone who finally decided to drink the poison first."

THE AUTHORS
IN ORDER OF APPEARANCE

AVRAH C. BAREN

Avrah C. Baren (she/they) is a SciFi/Fantasy writer based in the DMV, where she lives with a neurotic tuxedo cat. She is the author of *First Comes Death* and the editor/ contributing author for the *Of Stardust* anthology series. They spend their days researching mangroves and landcover change, and continue to nurse a passion for avian ecology. They love writing fantastical tales with Jewish-coded and explicitly Jewish characters that explore our connections with nature and each other. When she isn't writing, she is thrift shopping, working at the Renaissance Festival, and trying to become a wood witch. Find them on socials @avrahwrites or at abigailiswriting.com.

ROSE REGEANT

Rose Regeant is a writer, cat mom, and very tired teacher. She lives in Florida with her wife.

TALIA GREER

Talia Greer is the author of the paranormal monster romance novels Sasquatch Summer and Alder King Spring, and the romantic fantasy novel A Cure for Magic. She lives in the mountains with her gamer husband and two chaotic cat children. When she's not writing, she's drinking iced coffee or watching truly terrible horror movies. Talia can be found on Instagram and TikTok at @taliagreerbooks, and online at taliagreerbooks.com.

BEN MARIT

Ben Marit writes queer science fiction and fantasy about flawed people making bad decisions and somehow fighting through. He is a video game developer by day and lives in Texas with his partner and their spoiled rescue pup, Otis.

LILLIAN BARRY

Lillian Barry writes in short spells when the world stops spinning, which, when you have vertigo, isn't all that often. They write queer romance, including *The Santa Pageant* (2023; audio 2024). Lillian's non-bookish interests include playing brass instruments, watching anime, and getting sucked into the microcosm of a niche video game. A Channel Islander by childhood, they currently live in Ireland with their beloved partner. Find them @SoLillianBarry on social media.

HAILIE KEI

Hailie Kei (she/her), a lover of books and stories, writes an array of fiction including historical, fantasy, and YA contemporary. At the heart of all her stories are themes of immigration, belonging, and cultural identity—topics that play a big part in her own life as a British-Jamaican raised in the U.S. and living in Japan with her multi-cultural family. When she's not writing, she's managing iro.iro—a Discord server for BIPOC and Queer writers based in Japan.

D. E. OTT

D. E. Ott is a romance writer with a strong connection to the science-fiction fantasy stratosphere. She resides in South Florida with the towering palm trees, her beloved wife, and their nine noisy cats. When she isn't writing, she works full time as a high school English teacher, shaping the minds of what she hopes to be future literature fans. You can find D. on all of her socials @deottwriter

GABRIELLA BUBA

Gabriella Buba is a mixed Filipina-Czech author and chemical engineer based in Texas who likes to keep explosive pyrophoric materials safely contained in pressure vessels or between the covers of her books. She writes fantasy for bold, bi, brown women who deserve to see their stories centered. Her debut SAINTS OF STORM AND SORROW is a filipino-inspired epic fantasy out with Titan Books. DAUGHTERS OF FLOOD AND FURY to be released July 2025. Learn more at www.gabriellabuba.com or find her socials at @GabriellaBuba

VALO WING

Valo Wing (they/them) is a velvet blazer obsessed recovering operatic soprano turned professional funeral singer. Their short fiction is published in *Haven Speculative, Cosmic Horror Monthly, Brigids Gate Press,* amongst others, and was placed on the 2023 Nebula Awards recommended reading list. They are a 2021 Pitch Wars mentee and 2022 Futurescapes Writers' Workshop alum. They are represented by Laura Bradford at Bradford Literary Agency. Valo lives in Connecticut with their partner.